Stepbrother (An Alpha Stepbrother Romance)

By

Lillian Thorne

Copyright © 2015 Lillian Thorne
All Rights Reserved

All characters appearing in this work are fictitious. Any resemblance to real persons, living or dead, is purely coincidental.

TABLE OF CONTENTS

PART ONE
Chapter One
Chapter Two
Chapter Three
Chapter Four
Chapter Five

PART TWO
Chapter Seven
Chapter Eight
Chapter Nine
Chapter Ten
Chapter Eleven

Part Three
Chapter Twelve
Chapter Thirteen
Chapter Fourteen
Chapter Fifteen
Chapter Sixteen

Part Four
Chapter Seventeen
Chapter Eighteen
Chapter Nineteen
Chapter Twenty
Chapter Twenty-One
Chapter Twenty-Two
Chapter Twenty-Three

From the Author

Part One

Chapter One
Luke

I LIFT MY THUMB from the top of the straw I hold over my scotch and let a few drops of water fall into the glass, stopping after four. It's a delicate balance. Too much water and you risk diluting the scotch, but just enough and you release the subtle, floral notes hidden within it.

Not that it matters with the shit they serve here.

"Is there anything else I can do for you, sweetie?" The blonde bartender asks in a honeyed tone as she bends over the counter, placing her manicured hand on mine. She lets the question hang in the air as her fingers delicately trace my own. Her fake tits balloon under a revealing red flannel; glitter shimmers around her more than ample cleavage; the brim of her tan cowboy hat nearly touches my brow.

I could imagine her full pink lips wrapped around my hard cock, sliding back and forth. Under any other circumstances, I might make it happen; I might even enjoy it. But not tonight. Tonight I have more important things to deal with. I need to find Leah.

Sweetie? I repeat her words in my head. Her perfume, flowery and cloying, is starting to irritate me almost as much as her misplaced terms of endearment.

"You could grab me another scotch when I'm done." I tell her as I remove my hand from underneath hers, flicking the straw onto the counter as I turn around to face the main stage. She mutters *asshole* under her breath and stalks off toward the other end of the bar. She's probably right, but I can't help but smirk.

I sip my scotch as a fog machine blows puffs of gray smoke onto the stage. This isn't my scene. It's dark and dingy and reeks of smoke, dried sweat, and poor life choices. I'll need a shower after this; maybe burn my clothes.

A clone of the blonde bartender shakes her ass on stage while a motley of loud and lewd men shove filthy, crinkled dollar bills into her G-string. My jaw clenches as I picture Leah in place of the girl on stage— the same men pawing at her, attempting to fondle her tits and ass.

What forced her to work here of all places? She had so much potential. What a waste.

I pound the rest of my scotch and slam the glass down on the counter. The blonde bartender glares at me then turns back to the grimy guy she's milking cash from.

A part of me hopes I don't see Leah on stage while the other part is curious.

I squash the latter part as my eyes drift to a hot, curvy brunette in a dark corner of the room. My dick hardens as I see her bend over in tight daisy dukes and cowboy boots. Her flannel shirt stops mid-back and her perfectly shaped ass peeks out the bottom of her shorts.

"God damn." I exhale, leaning back against the bar.

I imagine my hands running over her silky thighs then grabbing fistfuls of that perfect ass. An urge overtakes me—a need to peel off those daisy dukes and feel her tight pussy clench around my hard dick. But she disappears and the moment is lost. For the best, I suppose. I need to find Leah and get her out of this place and this town.

I look back to the stage. Another girl has

joined the blonde, a petite redhead. They're making out. Classy. I can't help but respect their hustle though. They know what these men want, and they're willing to milk them for all they're worth. It's effective too.

Dollar bills are leaving hands quicker than water from a faucet.

I grab my glass and bring it to my lips but realize it's dry. I tap my ring against the glass to grab blonde number one's attention. She glances at me, and I wave my glass.

She snubs me. *Hell hath no fury...*

I consider leaning over the counter and grabbing a bottle myself, but decide against it. I sigh, fishing out a peace offering from my billfold, then wave it in the air like a white flag. I surrender. At least until I get another scotch.

Like a moth to a flame, she flies over to me in an instant.

"Scotch?" She asks as she rips the twenty from my fingers, turning around before I respond.

"Please." I smirk, watching her as she pours a couple of fingers of scotch into the glass.

She slams it down in front of me, scotch sloshing over the sides. I could reel her back in with a few kind words—it might even be fun—but I have more important shit to deal with at the moment.

"Thanks." My eyes narrow as I watch her walk away. Sometimes I can forget the simplest things. "Is Leah working tonight?"

She spins around and walks back to me. There's a certain bounce to her step now. She rests her forearms against the counter as she leans towards me. That same cloying smell flares my nostrils. I almost regret asking.

"What do you want with Leah?" Her voice takes on a more flirtatious tone as she smiles at me—a smile that tells me she thinks she's in control.

"That's not an answer." The scotch warms my throat as I swallow.

"Sure it is, honey." *Sweetie. Honey.* I can feel my chest flush. "It's just not the answer you're looking for."

"Well, is she—" I start, but I'm cut off by glasses and chairs crashing against the floor behind me.

"You fucking bitch!" I turn around and see a scrawny, scraggly-haired man, a bit shorter than me, shaking the brunette violently, her cowboy hat falling to the floor behind her. I can't see her face, but I can hear the squeals and pleas for help.

I drop my glass on the counter, about to intervene, but before I have the chance two bouncers swoop in and peel the guy away from her.

"You fucking whore!" The man spits at the girl as the bouncers drag him away.

The girl turns around, tears streaming down her cheeks, her face awash with confusion and sadness and distress.

I swallow hard.

It's Leah, my stepsister.

She has grown up and filled out—I hardly recognize her in that skimpy outfit—but there is no question about it; it's her.

My dick hardens as my eyes rake over her body. Chestnut curls, pouty lips, and delicate features—she's beautiful, absolutely stunning.

I'm losing focus, and I forget why I'm here as desire floods through me. I shouldn't be thinking like this. Not about Leah. I shut my eyes for a moment, but the very images I'm trying to suppress flash in my mind: thoughts of her naked body, my hands and lips exploring every inch of her silky skin.

When I open them again, Leah's gone.

CHAPTER TWO
LEAH

June 25th, 2013

I know the doctors told me to keep a daily journal—so did my dad. I know it's supposed to help me cope with my feelings, my urges. But I can't. Not every day. It's the same thing day after day. Writing the same entry every day makes me depressed, like my life is going nowhere.

Judith has retreated into her own world again. It's been hard since dad died. He was the only thing that kept me going these past few years. And I guess her as well. It was a shock to me when I heard. The news came a few days after he passed; I was still a patient at Millwood—sometimes I wish I still was.

Although I guess it wasn't that big of a shock. I watched as his health declined with each successive visit. He didn't know what was wrong, neither did doctors.

I was getting better while he was getting worse. It was heartbreaking. And during this time, Judith never visited me. Not once. The healthier I was, the more distant she became.

Luke never visited either. Not so much as a letter. Probably didn't even know I was at Millwood, or how he drove me there.

I hate him. I can feel heat flame up in the scar on my forearm every time I think about him. I don't want to admit it, but even though I hate him, he's the only person who cures my numbness, makes me feel something.

My poison. My antidote.

I have to leave this town. I need to get away. I feel myself slipping into old habits.

The headaches are back too. Some days my body aches so bad I can't get out of bed. Judith loves it though— taking care of me— but I can't stand it. The more unhealthy I become— the more torn up and broken I am — the more she cares for me. It's sick, it's twisted, and for some reason it keeps me here.

This place, my stepmother—everything here—is toxic.

Painful memories around every corner,

under every rock, yet I still stay.
My deepest fear is that I'll never leave.

ONE LOOK AT THE sea of drunk, wild men, hooting and hollering at Miley as she twirls around the pole, and I know it's going to be one of those nights.

My skin tingles. I snap the rubber band on my wrist against my skin. Relief.

I've been working at Buck Wild as a cocktail waitress for a few weeks now—two weeks exactly, actually. Without a college education and with my history, it's the only option I have.

When I first took this job, I thought I'd be insecure in my "uniform." I've never thought of myself as attractive or fit but after seeing how these men gawk at me, as gross and hideous as they are, I find myself becoming more confident each day.

Well, some days at least. Some days it's too much to handle, and I just want to run away and hide. Today is one of those days.

A few hours have passed and although I've had to deal with obnoxious drunk men and their lewd comments about my body, most of the men have been keeping their hands off. There's one guy who hasn't though, Gabe. He's a regular here—the girls put up with his shit because he tips well. I don't.

His greasy black hair, his slimy, yellow-toothed grin, and the way he invades my personal space—everything about him creeps me out. And his comments. Usually I let the catcalls slide off me, but there's something about the way he says them—maybe it's his voice—that makes my skin crawl. I want to gag just thinking about it.

Gabe signals me to come over. *Ugh.* I finger the rubber band around my wrist, pull it back—*Snap!*

I can smell his stench—booze, cigarettes, and B.O.—ten steps away.

"What can I get you Gabe, another Bud?"

He leers at me, not saying a word; his tongue slides over his yellow teeth. I fold my arms across my chest, trying to cover what I can.

"Say, it's been two weeks since you been here, right?" I hate the way he talks. His voice, how his lips curl, his shitty grammar—everything.

"Yes." I don't want to linger any longer than I have to.

"When we gonna see them titties on stage." I can feel his beady eyes burning on my cleavage. I raise my arm and snap my fingers in the air and wave in order to grab the attention of Mark and Greg, our bouncers. They're both leaning against the wall at the front, deep in conversation.

"You're drunk Gabe. I think it's best if you head home." I can feel myself growing more nervous and uncomfortable with every passing second. I quickly turn my head and look over my shoulder. Mark and Greg are still talking. The place is too loud, too dark. They can't see me.

"You think I'm gonna listen to what some whore tells me." His voice rises, grates against my ears. He's becoming belligerent. I need to leave. Now.

I turn away to walk towards Mark and Greg, but one of Gabe's bony hands shoots out and grabs my wrist, holding me in place. "I ain't done with you yet, slut." He slurs his speech as his grip tightens around my wrist.

Is this really happening right now?

He pulls me closer, the stench of tobacco and booze flares my nostrils, and I feel like gagging. He slides his free hand along my leg, and I try to shake it off, shake free from his grasp. Even though he's scrawny, he can still overpower me.

I notice a glass of water on the table within arm's reach. I grab the glass and dump it on his head while he's focused on my legs. The chair crashes to the floor, and I drop the glass, shattering it on the floor as he slides back from the table and grabs both of my wrists.

"You fucking bitch!" Specks of his saliva hit my face as he screams at me. My eyes are glued shut, and my head is turned to the side. *This isn't happening… this isn't happening.*

Everything around me seems to fade away, as though my body is shutting down. I can't think. I can't do anything. I'm lost.

Moments later his grip loosens, then releases me completely. I open my eyes and Mark and Greg are dragging him away. He mouths something, but I can't hear it. I'm in shock.

My cheeks feel warm, and I realize I'm crying silent tears, tears that tell me this is wrong, that I shouldn't be here. I look around me confused, dazed at what just happens. After a few moments, everything starts up again as though nothing happened.

No one gives a shit.

I run off to the back room, hoping there would be someone to talk with, commiserate with.

If you had asked me ten years ago where I'd be now, this wouldn't have even crossed my mind. A veterinarian, an art teacher, a housewife—something, anything but this.

I'm lost. I have been for years. Ever since Luke left.

A ship without a sail, a bird with a clipped wing. Damaged goods.

No one is in the back room. I find a corner and curl up into a little ball, trying to find some semblance of comfort. After a while, I heard someone speak.

"Leah, you okay?"

The voice seems distant. I feel a hand on my shoulder and I look up.

It's John, the owner of *Buck Wild.* If you saw him on the street—well you probably wouldn't, he'd blend in with the everyone else. Average. A balding, miserable middle-aged man.

I wipe away my tears, sniffle.

"Yeah, just fine." I lie.

My eyes sting. Beads of sweat glisten along his brow.

"Good," he continues, disregarding my tear-stained cheeks and the fact that I'm huddled in a corner, "I'm gong to need you on stage tonight."

I don't know how to respond—did he just say... "Excuse me?" I hardly recognize my voice. It's low and shaky but undercurrents of anger course through it.

"You knew this would happen eventually." He says it as though he's admonishing a child. "Tara and Vanessa are no-shows. Same with Becca. There's no one else. I need you to clean yourself up and get out there." His eyes scan my body. "You're a complete mess."

Something snaps. Not the rubber band against my wrist—something inside me. I've had it with this place, with this life.

"Fuck you." The words come out of me from somewhere deep inside me, low but firm. That gnawing anxiety in my chest disappears.

He stares at me blankly as I begin to rise. "What the fuck did you just say?"

I grab my purse, then walk up to him.

"I said fuck you and fuck this place. I'm fucking out." The words flow from me like water through a broken dam. It's exhilarating, freeing, everything I've ever wanted to say but never had to courage to.

Where was this person four years ago?

Still wearing my uniform, I turn to the door and start to walk.

"You walk out now and you're done." He reeks desperation (and cheese but whatever).

Without turning around, I raise my middle finger and push through the door. *Fuuuck. You*!

Chapter Three
Leah

I'm ecstatic. I can't remember a time that I've felt this amazing.

Unfortunately the feeling doesn't last long. Reality strikes hard as I'm standing next to my beater of a car, my key jammed in the lock. The more I twist, the more upset I become. My skin tingles, begging for release.

I can feel the tears forming. Resisting them is useless. I cry into the corner of my arm as I fall against my car. I just walked away from my ticket out of here. Sometimes I feel as though I sabotage myself on purpose.

Why couldn't I hold out just a bit longer?

"Look what he got here." My body numbs; I feel dizzy. There's a buzzing sound in my head. I don't have to turn around. I know who's behind me. I can smell his stench. "Look like the little whore run off and lost her way."

"Please…" I beg as I turn around, breathing in the cloying smells of alcohol and chewing tobacco and dried sweat. Blood drips from his nose, his lower lip split and dirty. Mark and Greg did a number on him, and he's not happy. The front of his mouth bulges with tobacco. He spits a dirty brown stream of saliva that lands in front of me before closing the gap between us.

"That's right, beg for it like a good little whore." His lips curl into a crooked smile, yellow and slimy. He's out for blood, and I'm out of my depth without Mark or Greg.

I look at the front doors of Buck Wild. They seem so far away. I could try to make a break for them, but I know I won't get far in these boots. Dread covers me like a cold sheet, and I scream. He shoves a hand over my mouth. It's salty and grimy and I feel like gagging.

"You'll shut that pretty little mouth of yours if you know what's good for you." I try to struggle, wriggle away from him, but Gabe's too strong, even for me. "Got it?"

He pins my right arm down against the car while my left swings wildly at him, blows glancing off him, his senses dulled by alcohol.

The more I struggle, the more he seems to enjoy himself.

"I like em' feisty." His eyes light up as his hand slides across my scar.

"So it's true. You goddamn crazy bitch." Flecks of his spit hit my face. His finger, blackened with grease and grime, traces the raised edge of the scar tissue as my heart hammers in my chest. He licks his lips.

"I bet you like it rough." He growls.

I try to beg him to stop, to leave me alone, but it all comes out muffled, unintelligible as his hand still covers my mouth.

He throws me to the ground, my hands and knees scrape hard against the asphalt, and I feel my skin burn. I can hear him unbuckling his belt, but I can't move; my body's stiff, frozen with fear.

"I'm gonna enjoy—"

He's cut off. I hear another pair of feet across the ground along with garbled, throaty noises. I turn my head and see the silhouette of another figure, one arm around Gabe's throat while the other holds it in place, tightening in a choke hold.

"You fucking done here?" The man's tone is confident, commanding, and it pulls on something inside me. It's familiar, but I can't place it.

Gabe struggles, trying to pry the man's arm away from his throat, his beady eyes bulging.

"You have five seconds to calm down." Gabe brings his boot hard against the man's shin, but it doesn't phase him.

"Alright then, sweet dreams." Seconds later Gabe goes limp, and the man sits him against a car.

It can't be.

My skin throbs and a sick feeling spreads outwards from my core.

"You okay, L?" The man says. He kneels down, and light strikes his face.

It's Luke.

The scar on my forearm burns and I reach for the rubber band, but he grabs my hand and pulls me to my feet.

I'm unsteady. My knees shake, the world spins around me, and I feel like a breeze could carry me away.

Why here? Why now?

I had imagined this moment for years, prepared for it even, but I never thought it would come. Not like this.

Of course it would happen like this. It

was Luke. Swoop in and be the hero. Maybe I'll forget about the pain he caused me when he left.

I shake off his grip. "What the hell are you doing here, Luke?"

"What? No, 'thank you'?" He tries to joke, but anger floods through me. "No hug, no kiss, nothing for saving you from captain creepy over there?" He nods to Gabe, groaning on the ground, his head swaying in circles as he's slowly coming to.

I push past him, my arm brushing against him as I try to open my car again.

"Oh come on Leah, you're not still mad are you?"

I turn around, jam my finger into his chest. I can feel the heat rise from my neck and chest, flood through my cheeks.

"Mad? Mad doesn't even skim the surface of what I'm feeling right now." He smiles. The same smile that made me melt when we were younger. It hasn't lost any of its power.

Flustered, I turn around and continue fiddling with the door. I feel Luke hovering behind me. His hand reaches around me, rests on my own. A chill runs through me and I close my eyes. I imagine the weight of his hand on my body, along my breasts and back, along my ass.

"Gentle." He whispers into the back of my ear, the warmth of his breath tickling the back of my neck. His voice is raspy, deeper and more sultry than I remember.

I feel him lean into me. *Is that…?*

The lock clicks and I snap out of my daydream. I scoot sideways as I open the door, sliding in without another glance at him. I can see him out of the corner of my eye, looming.

I'm scared. Nervous. I'm not ready to face him. The mix of emotions running through me tells me as much.

I snap my rubber band against my wrist but it's not working. Again. And again. I want to scream. I've been numb for so long; it's difficult to deal with this overwhelming flood of emotions.

I put the key in the ignition and twist—nothing. The battery is dead.

There's a light tapping on my window. I don't even have to look. I can feel the smirk from here.

I crank the window down, and Luke leans in, a half smile creeping on his face.

"Need a ride?"

"No."

"Are you going to wish yourself home?"

My cheeks flush. I hate how he mocks me.

"No. I'm walking."

He steps backward as I roll the window up, his arms folded under his chest. I can't help but notice his muscles bulging out of his t-shirt, veins snaking along his bicep, the way his pants cling to his muscular legs.

Even in plain clothes he's gorgeous.

Focus.

I try push by him but he grabs my wrist and pulls me into him.

"Come on. Don't walk away."

I'm dazed by his heady musk of cologne and bourbon and something else I can't place, but I recover.

"What, like you did?" I snap at him.

"Leah… That's not fair. I had to leave."

"No, you didn't!" Tears slide down my cheeks in tiny, meandering rivulets, warm and salty. All the emotions I thought I had under control flood through me. "You could've stayed!" Painful memories I've tried to bury flash in front of me: the empty bed; the kiss; the knife.

I shut my eyes and hope that when I open them again, it will be all a dream—a nightmare, I guess—something other than this. His warm hand gently smoothes my hair as he tries to soothe me. Every breath smells of him. My heart feels as though it's beating out of my chest.

"I know you don't believe me, but I can explain everything. I promise." I can feel myself softening as his deep, rich voice soothes me. I want to believe him. No matter how far he pushes me, he can always reel me back.

I hate him for it.

"Come on. Let me clean those cuts for you. I have a first aid kit in my car." He grabs my hand and drags me away before I have the chance to resist. I like how his large hand fits perfectly in mine, envelopes it completely, how he takes control when I can't.

He opens the door to his car, a white Mercedes-Benz G-Class. I wouldn't be able to identify any other Mercedes, or most cars for that matter, but this is the car that Luke always dreamed of buying one day. He had a picture of it in his room. I thought it was a silly dream, something all boys dream about but have no chance of achieving. But not Luke. Luke always had an incredible ability to make things happen.

Some people call it luck, but not Luke. Luke never believed in luck. He told me it cheapens all the hours of hard work he put in.

"Sit." He instructs me.

I sit down in the front seat, and run my hand along the cool, black leather while Luke is busy unwrapping bandages and alcohol swabs.

He did it. He actually did it.

So much time has passed since I've last seen Luke. I know so little about him now, his life, what he does. He's basically a stranger.

"So how'd you afford this?" I ask.

He ignores me, and I feel the sting of alcohol on my knee. *So much for being friendly.*

He places a band-aid on my knee, smoothes the adhesive with his hand. His touch lingers on my leg longer than it should, my skin tingling from his touch. I can feel his gaze on my legs, move slowly up towards my stomach, my chest, and eyes, then back down.

"Hand." He demands.

The scrape on my hand isn't very deep;

it doesn't need a bandage, but I want him to touch me, as wrong as that sounds.

I extend my hand, palm up, my scar out in the open. I can see him glance at it for a moment. I want to tell him: *See what you did. See what happened when you left?* But I can't.

As much as I want to blame him for it, deep down I know it was me who held the knife that day, not him.

His hair is inches from my face, and I can't help but breathe in his heady scent. I miss it. I miss him.

My heart hammers in my chest as he holds my hand gently in his, the other delicately tending to my scrape. His touch is tender, caring, and it's almost too much to bear as my feelings for him resurface.

Why am I doing this to myself? Why am I letting these feelings resurface? He left you once, and he'll do it again.

I rip my hand away as he finishes bandaging me.

"Are we done here?" I snap.

He looks up at me and smiles. I can feel myself flush, become anxious and nervous as his pale eyes dissect me. He can see through my act; he always could.

"Yes." He says simply, half amused. "Now buckle up. We're getting out of here." His eyes linger on mine, drift to my chest before flicking up to mine. I blush; he smiles. He turns around, walks to the other side of the car, and hops into the driver's seat. I'm still wearing my uniform, my breasts, my legs, my stomach—so much skin on display.

I should've grabbed my clothes, but I was in such a hurry to leave I forgot them.

It takes a moment for his words to sink in, but when they do… "Getting out of here? What do you mean?"

He takes a right out of the parking lot, the opposite direction from my house. He remains silent, eyes focused on the road.

"Luke!" I shove his arm, which is firmer, more solid than I remember, trying to get him to answer. He doesn't budge.

"You're not safe here."

I can't help but laugh.

"Okay…" I can see the muscles in his jaw clench and his right eyelid twitch, a nervous tic of his he has had forever. He's serious.

"Seriously, what's going on and where are you taking me?"

"To my apartment in Austin." He slows down for the stop light.

"You've been living in Austin this whole time? What the fuck is wrong with you?" I'm livid. He's living less than an hour away yet he never visited, never wrote, never tried to contact me once.

"Only recently. I have places all over the country." *Well good for you.*

He seems to be doing just fine without me. Fancy cars, slick clothes, and accessories. But why come back? Why now?

"And…?" I prompt. He ignored the first part of my question.

"And that's all you need to know."

I snort with laughter. Typical Luke—show up unannounced and expect everyone to drop everything on a whim and do exactly what he wants.

The. *Fucking*. Gall.

As I watch him drive, study his handsome features and muscled body, I realize why it always works, why everyone always bent over backward for him.

He's beautiful—absolutely gorgeous. I've watched girl after girl fall under his spell, listened to him fucking them as they screamed his name through our shared wall when we were younger. He always had a girl on his arm and a group of girls trailing not far behind, waiting for their chance with him.

I'd be lying if I said I didn't wish that I was one of them.

It was torture watching him burn through beautiful girl after beautiful girl. I became a loner because I learned early on that the only reason other girls hung out with me was to get closer to Luke. The first thing out of their mouths when they'd come over would be "So where's Luke?"

I hated him. I hated that I wanted him. But most of all, I hated that he still held this power over me years later.

Not anymore. I was putting an end to it.

"You know what? Fuck you, Luke! This is bullshit. You think you can just drop in after all these years without so much as a letter, a fucking phone call, and expect me to leave everything behind and follow you? And for what? You haven't told me shit except that I'm apparently in trouble. What the fuck sort of bullshit is this?"

Holy shit, did I just say that? I had never snapped like that before.

"What exactly are you leaving behind, Leah? A job at a strip club?" He nods to my uniform.

I finger the elastic band around my wrist, snap it against my skin without even thinking. The delicious sting spreads from my wrist, and I'm able to think clearly for a moment. I didn't want to admit it, but he was right. There was little left for me in this town; that's why I was working at a strip club.

He didn't have to be so harsh though.

"So you won't tell me why you're here?"

He nods. We're both silent for a moment, then: "You wouldn't believe me if I told you."

"Try me." He shakes his head and continues driving.

He was toying with me, playing another one of his silly little games. But I can't shake the nagging feeling in the back of my mind: There was something to this. He wouldn't show up after all these years to just play with me.

Even so, if he wasn't going to play fair, neither was I.

"Fine. If you're not going to tell me," I

say, folding my arms over my chest, "I'm not going."

"You act like you have a choice."

"I'll call the police. Tell them you kidnapped me."

He sighs. "No, you won't." He's right, I wouldn't.

"I'll call Miles." I can see his eyelid twitch and his grip tighten on the steering wheel. I think about his powerful hands around my wrists, pinning them above my head as he takes me.

Miles was a sore spot for Luke (for me as well but I don't want to get into that now). They were best friends when we were growing up, identical in nearly every way: star athletes, great students, heartthrobs—beloved by the community. They had a falling out when I started to see Miles; it was the first time I had ever seen Luke lose his temper. He was always in control, capable of bending any situation or anyone to fit his will.

But not Miles. Miles was different. At least, that's what I thought.

"Fine." Luke shrugs his shoulders, his knuckles still white as he grips the wheel. "If you don't want my help, that's your problem."

At the next red light, he leans over and reaches for my leg. I shift in my seat to move away from him, but his hand changes direction and opens the glove compartment instead.

"Something on your mind?" He asks with a smirk.

I ignore him.

He takes a pill from a bottle and swallows it, then puts the bottle back in the glove compartment. The light turns green and he makes a U-turn, heading toward our old house. It's not what I really want, but I can't stand him trying to control my life. He can't have everything he wants.

I smile as I consider telling him that. *That* would go over well.

We stay silent for a while. I have nothing to say and neither does he.

But then, just as we're nearing the house, I look at him again, at his strong, stubbled jaw and notice a few strange marks on his cheek. They run diagonally, three of them, and look like claw marks, like someone slashed him.

"What happened to your cheek?" I say, pointing to the marks. My question seems to catch him off guard, although I might be imagining it.

"I went and saw mom earlier today." He began.

"Wait what? Why?"

He hesitates for a moment but remains silent.

"She was in a mood. We both had some strong words for each other and she ended up slapping me. Her nails were pretty long and she scratched me as she pulled her hand away."

I wanted to press him, it seemed strange, but I didn't have the chance. We were pulling onto our street and it was lit with flashing lights—cop cars everywhere. There's a crowd on one side of the street, familiar and not-so-familiar faces.

Chapter Four
Leah

"What the fuck…" I mouth as Luke parks the car.

"Stay here." He says, as though I'd listen.

I open the door and follow him up the cement path to our house. The stairway to our porch is blocked off with police tape and a female officer intercepts Luke. Her black hair is pulled back in a pony tail revealing fine, vulpine features and hard green eyes.

"I'm sorry, but I'm going to ask you— Luke? Is that you?" Her stern expression fades and her eyes soften. *Ugh… who hasn't Luke fucked?*

Neither of them notice me brush by them, duck under the tape, and head up the steps to the house. *What is going on?* There's sick feeling growing inside me, gnawing at me.

A well-built officer is standing in the doorway with his back partly turned to me, writing something down on a clipboard. I try to sneak by him but he grabs me, but not before I see the body on the floor.

My stepmother. Dead.

Everything around me seems to fade, like I'm stuck in a vacuum, sucked into a black hole, a colorless void.

I'm sitting on the porch swing, the officer is telling me something but I can't understand him. He's kneeling down, has his hand on my shoulder. His lips are moving but I don't hear him. We're in two separate worlds.

There are so many questions buzzing around my head. I can't think. I close my eyes and let myself fall back into the swing; I let myself rock back and forth, back and forth. It's comforting, the rhythmic swinging, the cold air on my skin as my body moves back and forth.

When the initial shock wears of I realize that I'm not even crying. I'm not even sad. The pain I feel now is a fraction of a fraction of what I felt when my father passed away from a heart attack. There isn't any pain. In fact, I feel relieved. Relieved that she's dead. It may seem wrong but it's the truth.

After my real mom left and my dad married Judith, I thought that this would be my chance to have a real mother, someone who cared for me, who loved me. But it wasn't that way at all. Judith had this idea of a perfect daughter, how she looked, how she acted—everything. I could never live up to her expectations; I was never good enough for her. Her biting comments and passive aggressive actions made me even more insecure about my body and my self worth.

    I remember my first birthday as her stepdaughter. I had been wearing the same clothes for years and they were quickly becoming too small. She bought me a completely new wardrobe—I was so excited. But that excitement disappeared as I began unwrapping the presents, each one holding clothing more than a couple sizes too small. "Well… maybe in a few years dear." She had a way of saying things, soft and wistful, as though I had disappointed her. She locked herself in her room and didn't come out until the next day. Even then, she didn't acknowledge me or what happened the day before.

    Living with her was hell. It didn't help that I was almost always sick, in and out of doctor's offices, hospitals—new treatments each month. No one had a clue what was wrong. I think it had something about that old house: that's when it all started—a few months in. The only positive being that Judith always wanted to take care of me when I was sick. I don't know why, but it seemed as though the sicker I became, the more attached and motherly she would become. Over the years I became numb, a shell of a person.

Luke tried to help me get through it, deal with her, but he wasn't always there. When he was distracted with other girls and things I had to find my own coping mechanisms. I turned to cutting. It worked for a while, but it only gave me a brief escape from my reality, never truly fixed anything. And in the end, it tore me apart.

When I finally come back to reality, I realize someone draped a blanket around me. I cling to it's warmth, it's security. I look around, the lawn is buzzing with cops walking in and out, some milling around chatting. Luke was still talking with the female officer from earlier. I couldn't see his face, but I could see her's. Her cheeks were rosy, warm from laughter, a smile stretching wide across her face and dimples on her cheeks. She was obviously smitten, and I was obviously jealous. Heat rose from my chest. I hated how effortlessly he attracted women. Including me.

"Can I get you anything else Leah?" I nearly jump. Lost in my world, I didn't realize someone was sitting next to me.

I turn my head, and my breath catches in my chest.

It's Miles.

The only thing about him that hasn't changed is his eyes, a swirl of green and brown that comes close to hazel, but not quite.

"Miles?" My voice wavers in the air.

"Yes, Leah. Miles" He smiles at me. A reassuring smile that puts me at ease. But not for long. His face awakens a memory, one that I've tried to bury. Images flash in my mind in rapid succession: the woods; the fallen tree; the kiss. I close my eyes, try to focus on something, anything other than my broken memories.

A tear rolls down my cheek. "Leah, everything is going to be okay." He puts an arm around me. It's big, warm, and comforting. "I promise." He wipes away the tear with his thumb, a tear that he probably thinks is for Judith. But it's not.

"What happened?" I ask, meekly.

"We're not sure yet."

"What do you mean?" I ask, knitting my eyebrows.

He sighs, places his hand on my shoulder. A chill runs through me.

"There's not a lot I can say right now." He's deflecting, hiding something.

I sigh. It's been a long day and I just want to sleep. I can feel his eyes burning on my skin.

"Look, I probably shouldn't be asking you this." A ghost of a smile flashes on his face. "But do you need a place to stay? I have an extra bedroom. And—" I don't have a chance to respond, Luke steps in.

"You're right. You shouldn't be asking that." He reaches down and grabs my arm. "She's staying with me." He pulls me to my feet effortlessly, like I'm a child's plaything.

Tense energy vibrates between the two of them as they size each other up. Miles stands up, his nose inches from Luke's. I can feel Luke's grip tightening on my arm and I squeal. He lets me go and I rub my wrist.

"Luke." Miles says with a grin. "I heard you were back in town."

"Really?" Luke responds, amused. "And

where'd you hear that?"

Miles nods over Luke's shoulder, and both of us look. Mrs. O'Malley, the widow who lives next door. Her bony fingers grab tightly at her knit shawl as she talks with two officers. She looks distraught, her gray hair wild. Although, now that I think about it, she usually does. But more so than usual, I guess.

"She has a few interesting stories."

"Most drunks do."

Miles folds his arms under his chest, tips his head back and to the side, studying Luke, analyzing his demeanor. Luke snorts with laughter, and for a moment, the tension that was building is alleviated. He extends his hand.

"Good to see you again, Miles." But the forced smile on Luke's face says "Fuck you."

Miles turns to me, snubbing Luke's handshake, and pulls out a card. "Call me. Let's talk." He was serious.

Luke grabs the card from him before I have the chance to react. "Will do."

"What's that on your cheek, Luke?" Miles asks just as Luke was turning away. Luke hesitates for a moment, looks at me and then turns to Miles.

"Just a scratch."

"Looks like a little more than that."

Luke grabs my arm and pulls me away.

"Luke." Miles calls from behind us. Luke stops, but doesn't turn around. "You might not want to wander very far."

We're in front of the door. I can't help but look inside. The body's gone. *The body. She hasn't been dead for more than a few hours and I'm referring to her as 'the body.'*

"You know how to reach me." He tugs at my arm and continues down the stairs.

"Wait," I protest, trying to pull myself away from him, "I need to grab some clothes."

"We'll get you some at my place." He says, brushing me off. I can feel myself heating up. I dig in my heels, tear away from him.

"Fine, but I'm not leaving without Crouton." Crouton's my cat, a large tabby that I've had for ages and I'm not about to leave here without him. I can see Luke's jaw clench, his muscles tighten as he looks at the street in front of him. I can see Mrs. O'Malley peering nervously at us from behind the two officers. She makes eye contact with me, then looks away.

"Luke." I say, more calm, more assertive.

"You know I'm allergic." *I do… but who will feed him? I'm not above throwing a temper tantrum right now.* He let's go of my hand, sighs. "Fine." *Yes!*

I squeal, run up and jump on him, hugging him. "Thank you thank you thank you!"

"He stays in your room. You keep him in there. Door shut. If I see him out I'll get rid of him." I can feel his strong arms tighten around me as he holds me. His left hand slides down my spine to my lower back, warmth penetrating my core, but then he lets go and I run back up to the house.

"Can I grab Crouton?" I ask Miles. His body language is closed, arms folded across his chest, head bowed almost to his chest; I can sense he was watching us, but he has a smile when he looks at me.

"Crouton?"

"My cat." He stares at me a moment, as though amused with something.

"Of course. I'll grab him."

I peek inside while Miles disappears upstairs. Everything looks the same, but it feels eerie. I'm not sure what to make of it. I watch a tall, slender officer with a mop of black curls place his camera into a black bag and sling it over his shoulder. The laminate I.D. card hanging from his neck swings side to side as he walks toward the door, toward me. He can't be much older than I am. He gives me a half smile as he passes by. He reeks of cigarettes and body spray.

Miles returns with Crouton not much later. Our fingers graze each other's when he hands me the carrying case. Crouton whines, claws through the holes in the side of the case in protest.

I thank Miles and turn to leave. I'm halfway down the stairs when he calls out.

"I meant what I said. If you need a place to stay…"

I smile politely at him, but keep moving. I'm not ready to face my past.

Most of the commotion from earlier has died down. Cops are packing up, crowds dispersing, and I'm ready to follow suit. As I'm walking to Luke's car, I see the tiny, shawled figure of Mrs. O'Malley standing next to it pointing and yelling at Luke. I can't hear what she's saying, but Luke seems not to be paying any attention to her.

In fact, it looks like he's amused. Although I might be imagining it: it's too dark, and he's too far away.

By the time I make it to the car, another officer—the one who was flirting with Luke earlier—has taken Mrs. O'Malley by the arm and is trying to calm her down. Her face is bright red and puffy, tears stream through the deep wrinkles around her cheeks and mouth. I'm not sure how old Mrs. O'Malley is. She was living next door to us when we moved in, but she seems just as old now as she did back then. She was always nice to me; It's sad to see her this distraught.

I can make out fragments, bits and pieces of her incoherent rant. She points to Luke, then turns to me and before I have a chance to react, she lunges at me with amazing quickness and dexterity for a woman her age and stature and grabs me by the arm. I nearly drop Crouton. His case swings in my hand but I hold on.

Her eyes are wide, fierce and clear. "Run." She rasps, bowing her head as the officer pulls her away and escorts her home. I'm frozen in place trying to figure out what just happened. Luke rolls down the window.

"You coming?" He's brusque, irritated

by something. *What the hell did I do?*

"Yeah."

I wasn't in the car long before I figure it out.

"Don't talk to Miles." *Great… here we go again.*

He's jealous, defensive, as though someone else is encroaching on his territory. It seethes from him, through his voice. The way he's gripping the wheel, I'm surprised he hasn't crushed it yet.

"What makes me think you can tell me what to do?" I push back. His jaw clench, then relaxes.

"You'll do as I say if you want to stay with me." And there it is. There's always some caveat with Luke. If you want x then you better do y for me. And he knows I have no other option. I have no money, no friends, no where to go. There's Miles's offer, but I'm not so sure I'd be better off with him.

"I saw the way he was staring at you." He snarls, continuing with his rant. "He's unprofessional. A creep." He says it as though he hasn't been looking at me the same way. I noticed it the first times our eyes met, when his hand lingered on my leg longer than it should have when he was bandaging the scrape on my leg.

"And officer fake tits was any more professional? I'm surprised you haven't fucked her yet."

"Who says I haven't?" I could feel myself flush. He always finds a way to weasel his way under my skin. I snap the band around my wrist. Again. And again.

"Why do you keep doing that? That thing with your wrist?"

I ignore him.

We're silent the rest of the way.

Chapter Five
Leah

An hour later and we're at his apartment, a penthouse in the heart of downtown Austin. Moonlight streams through floor to ceiling windows, dapples the sleek grey furniture and hardwood floors. It's refined, elegant, like nothing I've ever experienced before. My mouth is dry—it's been wide open since pulled into his private garage, rode his private elevator to the top floor and opened the cold, metal door of his apartment.

I set Crouton's case down on the floor, open the front to let him out. He sniffs cautiously at first, pokes his head out and then shoots off down a dark hallway.

"Remember our deal." Luke says sternly as he tosses his keys into a basket next to the door. "Keep him in your room."

"Sorry. I'll go grab him." I don't know why I was apologizing. It's not like I wanted to be here. Luke basically forced me. He loves to control other people and I hate that I allow him to do it to me.

"The guest bedroom is the second door on the right, just down the hallway," He says, pointing the same direction in which Crouton scampered off. He's moving around —nervous energy—picking things up, throwing things away, turning on lights and switches, putting things in order. "It's a mess. I'm sorry. I left in a hurry." I look around and can't see the mess he's talking about. The apartment feels sterile, clinical almost, as if it hadn't been lived in.

It's been a long day. So much happened and I just don't know how to react to it all. I should feel sad, angry—something—but I just feel numb. I want to hold Crouton. Just fall asleep and forget everything. But I know it isn't that simple. It never is.

"You're probably tired." Sometimes I feel he can read my thoughts. He walks over to me; I can feel an intense energy surge between us. It's the first time I've had the chance to look at him, really look at him since he's been here.

He's gained weight. Not in a bad way— he's more muscular, filled out. His face, like the rest of his body, is lean. He moves with confidence and grace, with purpose. My nostrils flare as his scent reaches me, floods my senses. "You should probably get some rest." My heart skips a beat as his hand cups the left side of my face, warmth radiating from his touch. Butterflies flutter in my stomach. I look into his eyes, pale blue in the moonlight, then to his lips. I imagine them on mine, but I shake off the thought.

"I don't know what I'm going to do." I say. I can feel tears building, but I hold them back.

"You'll stay here with me."

A part of me wants to, it craves him, his touch—closeness. But the other, more rational part of my brain can't help but chime in: *He left you once, what makes you think he won't do it again? Tread lightly… you don't want to end up at Millwood again."*

"I can't stay here forever."

"Of course, but a week wouldn't hurt, right?" *I'm not so sure.* He lets go of me, and walks towards the kitchen. "Besides, circumstances… have changed." He opens a bottle of water, takes a sip, and sets it down on the counter. Then looks at me, hoping that I take the bait. I've played this game before. He wants me to beg, plead with him to explain what he means. He's just toying with me, offering vague bits of information he has no desire to elaborate. I won't indulge him.

"Fine. Whatever." I pull away from him. "Where's the bathroom?"

"First door on the left." He points down the hallway, then takes another sip of water. I can feel his eyes follow me as I pass by him. "I'll put a change of clothes on your bed."

I walk down the hall, open the door to my room and find crouton curled up in a ball on my bed. I feel his soft fur in my hand, stroking him gently as he purrs with approval.

I leave Crouton alone on the bed and find my way to the bathroom. The room fills with steam as water streams down my body. Flowery soaps and scrubs and body washes litter the shower and I wonder how many women he's fucked in here. I can't stay here —it's not right. Every second I'm near him I find myself being drawn to him, pulled to him by some invisible force I have no control over. As much as I hate to admit it, I like it. I like how he affects me—how I can actually feel *something* when I'm with him.

It's why I started cutting: to feel something, to get rid of the numbness.

But that's why I have to leave. It's not right, my feelings for him. Besides, it's not like he'd ever feel the same way about me. How could he? He could have girl he wants. I've watched how women fawn over him, unabashedly throw themselves at him. Why would he ever want me?

I have to leave. I can't face another heartbreak, and I can't rely on Luke to help cure this numbness.

I turn off the shower, wrap myself in a towel and head to my bedroom. The apartment is dark except for the light filtering into the hallway from Luke's bedroom, the door cracked open. I push open the door to my room.

Before I have a chance to react Crouton bolts out of the room and down the hallway. "Crouton!" I yell as he weaves in and out of other rooms.

Crazy cat mode: engage. Why does it have to happen now?

He's sitting at the end of the hall, staring at me, his tail twitching as though he's asking me if I want to play this game of his. No is my obvious answer, but unfortunately for me I have no way of getting that across to him.

"Crouton!" My voice is low but strained. "Get. Over. Here." I wave at him, hoping by some miracle he'll follow me. "Now!" But he remains steadfast, staring at the funny-looking human in a towel, waving her arms like a madwoman. I groan as I trudge reluctantly over to him. Just as I'm reaching down to grab him, he spins around and dashes through the door behind him, forcing it to swing open a hair wider. But that's just enough.

I look up and see Luke, bent over as he's pulling on his boxers. He's naked and I can't tear my eyes away from him. His legs, his arms, his torso—every part of his body—looks as though he were chiseled from marble, a representation of a Grecian ideal. My core floods with heat, my mouth hangs open. His cock hangs between his legs, thick and long and hairless. He's looking at me, the corners of his mouth curl up slowly into a smile.

And it's then that I realize I've dropped my towel.

My breath catches in my chest and I feel a shock jolt through my body. I grab the towel, clutch it tightly against my chest and turn to run. "Sorry!" I yell over my shoulder as I sprint down the hallway to my room.

Stupid, stupid cat.

It feels as though my entire body is on fire as I shut the door behind me.

I want to scream. I need release. I finger the rubber band around my wrist. *Snap*—calm slowly returns, my breath less ragged. No big deal, right? *Ugh!* I want to curl up into a ball and die.

I let the towel fall to the floor and I find a pair of grey sweatpants and a crisply-folded white shirt that Luke laid out for me. I slip both on and fall into bed. It's soft and warm and the duvet feels like silk against my skin. I look down at the scar on my forearm, touch it for the first time in years. It pulsates under my touch.

Remember, I tell myself, *remember what he pushed you to and how far you've come. Don't stop now. Don't let him—*

The door cracks open. I pretend to be asleep—it's silly, I know. No one can fall asleep that fast, especially after seeing what I just saw. My eyes are tight, but I can feel his presence over me, his scent, his energy.

Crouton hops on my bed and Luke

sneezes.

"Bless you." I say instinctively, immediately wishing that I could reach out and take it back. I cringe at how stupid I can be.

"Thanks." He says. I don't have to see him to know that he's smirking at me. "Can I get you anything? Are you comfortable?"

"I'm fine…" I groan into the pillow.

"Hey… It's okay." He sits down on the bed next to me and places his hand on my shoulder, rubbing it through the duvet. "I know that it must've been your first time seeing a man naked." My cheeks flush. *Oh… my god.* "I'm sure you're wondering about what you're feeling right now, but don't worry, it's natural. Completely normal."

Fireworks explode in my head. The room may be dark but I'm seeing red.

I spring up and start slapping his body. "That's. Not. Funny." I say as he's sitting there laughing, obviously amused with himself.

"It's a joke!" He wraps his arms around me so I can't move. "Calm down. It's just a joke."

His heady scent overwhelms my senses

again, and my body relaxes in his embrace. I feel myself melting into him. My body tingles in his arms, in his firm grasp. His hand slides down my spine, rests on my lower back, heat penetrating my core, throbbing, aching—wanting for his touch, to feel his hands all over my body. I don't care how wrong it is.

He pulls back, looks me in the eyes. At this distance, they're a pale grey, and I can see them flood with lust. His right hand moves to my cheek and I rub my face against it, turn and breathe in his scent before looking again into the pale fire growing in his eyes.

Kiss me. Just kiss me.

I bite my lower lip, waiting. Waiting. But the moment never comes. His hand falls from my cheek and he leaves me alone on the bed. The air in front of me still buzzes with his energy and scent—a specter of him.

"Goodnight." He says, then closes the door behind him.

I try to fall asleep, but I'm too wired. I'm not like him. I can't push these feelings away so easily. I can't run away from everything like he did. I toss and turn, tortured by my thoughts of Luke, the moment we shared. Am I making it out to be something more than what it was? I don't know, but I can't stop thinking about it, or him.

His perfect body. His perfect lips. His intoxicating scent that still lingers in the air.

I slip my hand underneath my pants, my breath hitching as my fingers slide over my wet mound. I finger myself, thinking about Luke until I come.

Only then does sleep cover me.

CHAPTER SIX
LEAH

CROUTON IS SCRATCHING AT the door when I wake up. I check the clock: 12:14 PM. It's late. Much later than I normally get up. It was a long day and even longer night, so it's not unexpected.

I bend over and scratch his ears. "You must be hungry!" I say to him as I open the door. "I promise I'll—"

He shoots out without looking back. "Find you some food..." I finish.

The apartment looks so foreign in the daylight, and I feel like an intruder, and unwelcome guest among the high-end furnishings. Luke's gone. I see Crouton sunning himself by the window on the opposite end of the apartment.

I look in the fridge for something to eat, but nothing looks appealing. My appetite is non-existent. I sink into one the the leather couches and decide to watch some television, but the remote has far too many buttons and I have no desire to fiddle around with it. So instead, I decide to explore Luke's apartment. If I'm going to be living here for a while, I might as well know where everything's at.

There's a door opposite my bedroom that has been closed since I've been here. Every other door is wide open except for this one. I turn the knob and push the door open, peering inside. It's dark, and I can't see much—there aren't any windows from what I can tell. The room smells of paint and chemicals, and my attention is so focused on the dark room in front of me that I didn't hear Luke come in. I bolt upright as he pushes in front of me and shuts the door, then locks it from the outside.

He offers no explanation, just walks around me and lays a few bags on the kitchen counter. "I picked up some things for Crouton."

I walk over to him and find cat food and litter and toys and an assortment of other goodies for Crouton. "Wow! Thank you so much." I didn't think he could be this thoughtful. It's a welcome surprise. His scent reminds me of the night before, and before I have to chance to stop myself, the words are already out.

"About last night…" I begin, let the words hang in the air hoping that Luke will finish.

"Don't worry about." I couldn't help but worry about it. I felt something, and I can't ignore it, walk away from it like Luke walked away from me years ago. "You hungry?"

I can't believe he's acting so… normal. As though his mom didn't just die, as though he didn't just reappear in my life, as though we didn't see each other naked last night. Or that we were moments away from kissing… It's strange and infuriating and I can't let it go.

"What are you doing? *What* exactly is going on?"

"I'm making eggs. Would you like some?" He says with a smile, raising the carton of eggs up for me to see.

"That's not what I meant. What are *you* doing? Why did you bring me here?" I can feel myself getting more annoyed with him. He never took anything seriously, yet he was always the best at everything. It was so frustrating living with him. It *still* is.

"Well, where else were you going to go?" He cracks a few eggs into a pan, then tosses in a lump of butter.

"That's not what I mean. You know that. You wanted to take me away before…" I didn't want to say her name. "You know. *It* happened."

"Don't worry. In time. Right now it's time to eat. Do you know what makes a good scrambled egg?" He asks, pointing a spatula at me, deflecting the conversation elsewhere. He was good at that. I didn't want to indulge him but I'm sure he was going to tell me whether I wanted to know or not. I groan, apparently his cue to keep going.

"Control." The word hangs in the air, his voice firm and his eyes on mine. "You have to control the heat." I can see the muscles in his back ripple under his shirt as he adds butter and a few eggs to the pan. My mind returns to last night. "Keep stirring. When the eggs begin to solidify, off the heat, but keep stirring." I feel his hand against my cheek, the way his eyes looked at me—their fierceness, flooded with lust. "Back on the heat. Stir. Stir. Stir. Control." I want him to control me, hold me, take me. "Then back off the heat. Season… and serve."

My hand unconsciously touches the back

of my neck, moves down across my chest as I close my eyes and continue my fantasy. I can feel the warmth of his breath against my cheek, his scent.

The clang of plates jolts me from my fantasy. Luke scoops the eggs out of the pan and onto a plate, then sets it down in front of me.

"Enjoy." He says, smiling down at me.

My eyes light up when I take my first bite. They're the most delicious eggs I had ever tasted, creamy and salty and absolutely perfect. I won't tell him that though—don't want to inflate his ego any more than it already is. But of course Luke would be able to cook like this. What couldn't he do?

"So are you going to tell me why you dropped in out of the blue?"

"You really want to know, huh?" He kneels down beside me and places a hand on my knee, sending a chill down my spine as goosebumps erupt along my arms.

I look at him blankly.

"Fine. If you really want to know—"

His phone rings and he walks over to the counter to answer it. *Ugh.* His demeanor changes, he seems tense, agitated, and his responses are curt.

"Sure. Today? Fine. What time? Fine." He hangs up and tosses his phone onto the couch. He grabs a cup from the cabinet, fills it with water and downs it in one gulp.

"What was that about?" I ask, looking at him then back down at my eggs, picking away at them with my fork.

"Miles. I have to go down to the station."

"Why?"

"I was the last one to see my mom alive."

Before Luke leaves, he drops a leather-bound notebook on my lap. "It was Robert's." Robert was my dad, *is* my dad.

"I know that, but how did you get it? Not even I knew were he kept it and—"

"It doesn't matter." He cuts me off, still agitated. He takes a deep breath, adding more calmly: "I have a few sections marked, read them. They'll tell you everything you need to know."

"Okay…" Is all I can manage before he turns to leave. Nothing in the past 24 hours has made much sense to me.

The door shuts as I flip to the last bookmarked page.

There's a single sentence. No date. I recognize the handwriting as my father's. The sick feeling in my stomach spreads throughout my body. I'm dizzy, light-headed and I feel like passing out. My limbs grow numb as I read the sentence again and again, hoping that it changes.

But it doesn't.

Something other than myself takes control and I find myself in the kitchen, a knife in front of me on the counter. The blade is cold and sharp as my finger slides over it. The need for release consumes me, and I'm not sure I can resist this time.

Part Two

Chapter Seven
Luke

Mile's office is nothing special: a small, windowless box lined with metal filing cabinets. The air is warm and stagnant and smells of stale coffee and cigarettes. Random piles of shit clutter the floor and tops of cabinets; cardboard boxes with cockeyed lids spew papers.

A small clock hanging on the wall above the door ticks time away while the low hum of conversation trails into the office.

I'm sitting on a hard plastic chair, the kind of chair you might find in a high school classroom. I'm sure if I reach my hand underneath it I'll find gobs of discarded gum stuck to the bottom. It's tempting, but I think I'll pass.

I cross my right leg over my left and lace my fingers together on my knee as I watch Miles shuffle papers behind the stacks of files and folders and refuse that litter his desk. At least, I can only assume a desk is hidden underneath it all. His shirt is freshly-pressed, his face clean-shaven, and his black hair well-groomed; he seems strangely out of place amidst the chaos of his office.

The crisp sound of paper rubbing against paper fills the office as Miles pretends to be busy and interested in what's written on the pages. He's been at it for the past 15 minutes: reading files, opening drawers, pulling things out, writing things down. Wasting my time. He's trying to get me to lose my cool. It won't work. I'll play along, let him think he's in control. It's a fun little game, and I never lose.

I fold my arms across my chest as I lean back in the chair and close my eyes. Images of the night before flash in my mind. I see Leah's naked body sprawled out on the bed, so perfect, so beautiful. I can smell her sweet scent, recall the feel of her silky skin under my hands, and how all of it led to the moment I nearly gave in to my urges, ripped off the thin fabric that separated her body from mine and claimed her.

I know she's my stepsister, but there's something about her that drives me wild… I can't control myself.

My dick hardens as I continue to think about her flawless body: the way her daisy duke's clung to her perfect ass; the swell of her breasts underneath her red flannel shirt. When I first saw her in that uniform at Buck Wild, I wanted to bend her over and take her from behind, feel her tight little hole clench against my dick. I still do.

I shake myself out of the fantasy. I'm getting too close. I'm letting her in and that can't happen. I'm no good for her. She's innocent, pure. I'll only warp her, twist her into something else, something wrong. We're wrong. What happened last night was a mistake—a small lapse in judgment. It won't happen again. It *can't* happen again.

A sigh escapes me as I pull out my cell phone to check my email. Miles's eyes shift from the files to me. He looks at me as though I hadn't been sitting here for the past 15 minutes.

"I'm sorry." He grins at me, a shit-eating grin, before dropping the files on the desk. "I completely forgot you were here. Laser focus. I'm sure you understand." A half smile forms on my face; I understand alright. "Would you like something to drink before we start? Water? Coffee?"

"No, thanks." I want to get this shit done. I clear my throat as I shift my weight in the chair. My ass is growing numb sitting here.

Miles stands up, turns around and grabs a glass carafe from the shelf behind him and pours room temperature coffee into a white ceramic mug. "Sugar and cream?" he asks.

I applaud his effort. He's *really* trying. He might make a mediocre detective one day. I say nothing.

"Yeah, I'm not a fan either. Black. That's the only way." He grins at me, placing the mug in front of me as he walks toward the door to his office. It clicks shut and he heads back to his desk.

"So." He begins, sitting back down, the chair creaking under his weight. He clasps his hands in front of him and rests his forearms on the edge of his desk. "I just want to thank you for coming in today on such short notice, but I appreciate your cooperation with this investigation." His hands bob to the cadence of his speech.

It's an investigation now… interesting.

"And I'm truly, truly sorry for you loss." Bullshit. He knew Judith, saw the shit Leah and I dealt with on a daily basis. This wasn't a loss, and he wasn't sorry. Judith had it coming.

"Not a problem." I grit my teeth. With the door shut, the room begins to feel like a sauna.

"How's Leah holding up? She's had a rough few months." *Months? He has no idea.*

"Fine." I say brusquely; I'm growing tired of this chit chat.

He looks at me for a long moment, then nods. "If you don't mind, I'd like to begin."

"Sure."

He grabs a small black tape recorder, places it in front of him and clicks it on. Then he grabs a pen and a pad of paper. His eyes harden as he looks at me. "What can you tell me about last night?"

I tell him about last night. Some of it true, some it false. Mostly false. He doesn't need to know the whole story. It doesn't matter much anyway.

"Uh huh." He says, stroking his chin with his thumb and index, mulling over what I just told him. He leans toward me; I can see beads of sweat form along his brow and upper lip. "I still don't understand why she… why your mom would attack you." He points to the marks on my cheek.

I shrug. "Neither do I." Lie. "She wasn't

the most stable person, as you know." Truth.

"She seemed stable and lucid the last time we spoke." There's a tinge of irritation in his voice. It's subtle, but it's there. He clears his throat.

"Mrs. O'Malley overheard you two in a heated argument. Spooked her. Do you recall what that argument was about?" He leans back and takes a sip from his cup without taking his eyes off my face.

Why can't he just give up? My shirt begins to cling to my skin as wet spots form across my chest and back. The heat is getting to me. These questions are getting to me. This is a fucking waste of time.

"Do you believe everything a drunk says?" I snap at him.

His lips curl into a smile. I take a handkerchief out of my pocket and dab my forehead. I shouldn't have said that. I shouldn't lose my temper.

"Sorry," I say more calmly, taking a deep breath. "The heat is getting to me."

"No A/C." He waves a hand in front of him. "I get it."

"I wouldn't call it a heated argument." I continue.

"Do you recall what the conversation

about then?"

"Money, I believe." Another lie.

"What about money?" His eyes lit up. It caught his interest. Good.

"She wanted a loan and I wouldn't give her one. She has—" I take a deep breath, let it out. "...*had* a pill addiction and I wasn't about to fund it." Partially true.

"I see." He leans back and folds his arms below his chest, staring at me blankly. I know Miles well enough to recognize that he's not convinced. We used to be close back in high school, but after what happened... Well, let's just say neither of us goes out of our way to be friendly with each other.

I take my phone out and glance at the time. I wonder how much of the journal Leah has read by now—whether or not she can connect all the dots. It's a lot of information to take in at once. I hope she's okay.

"Don't worry, I won't hold you here much longer." The right side of his mouths curls into a half smile. "One last question. If you don't mind, of course." He asks as though I have a choice.

"Go on."

"When Judith attacked you, did you retaliate? Harm her in any way?"

There must have been a bump on her head when she fell.

I frown. "Retaliate? Is that a joke?"

"You don't have to answer." He says, raising his eyebrows.

I run a hand through my hair as I look down at the floor.

"No," I say, looking back up at him, making sure my voice is level, smooth. "When she came at me, I grabbed her wrists to restrain her. She was kicking and screaming and spitting. I wanted to calm her down. But then she bit me." I pull back my sleeve and show him a purplish bruise on my arm. He cringes.

"You might want to get that checked out."

"Anyways," I say, continuing with the story. "After she bit me, I pushed her away from me. She lost her balance, fell backward and hit her head on a cabinet. Just a bump, nothing serious. She got back up almost immediately."

I could feel myself flush. I reach into my pocket and pull out a pill. "Mind if I have some water?"

"Sure." Miles leaves the office and returns with a small Dixie cup filled with water, handing it to me.

I swallow the pill as Miles sits back down. He stares at me as I crush the Dixie cup and toss it in the waste bin by the door. It rims in. Still got it.

"She had more than a little bump on her head, Luke." He says, cocking his head slightly.

"What do you mean?" I can feel my face involuntarily contort with a mix confusion and uncertainty.

He takes a deep breath and stands up. The leather soles of his shoes click against the floor as he walks behind me and grabs a baseball from on top of a cabinet. I listen as he tosses it in the air and catches it, leather smacking against bare skin. He does this a few times before replacing it. He turns the chair next to mine toward me and sits down, his elbows on his knees and his hands clasped in front of him. I meet his gaze.

"She had a significant wound on her head. She lost a lot of blood. That's what I'm saying, Luke." There's tension in his voice, restrained anger. Color spreads from his neck, along his jaw and up his cheeks.

"She was fine when I left." He stares at me blankly, not saying a word. He shrugs, then leans back in his chair. "Is that what killed her? Blood loss?" I ask.

"Still looking into it. All we know is that, as of now, you were the last one to see her alive."

"I've told you all I know." Lie.

"We're going to have to search you car." He says abruptly.

"For what?" I snap.

"Look. We don't know what happened to your mother. We're trying to explore every avenue available. I'd appreciate it if you cooperated." If I cooperated… What the fuck was I doing right now? I didn't have to come here.

"Fine. Search my car." I take my keys out of my pocket and toss them on a pile of folders on his desk. He's not going to find anything.

"Thanks." There's that shit-eating grin again. "Speak with Jessica on your way out. You can borrow a car."

I stand up to leave.

"We'll be in touch."

I find Jessica, grab the keys, and leave in a rusted piece of shit that sputters and whines all the way back to Austin.

IT'S DARK BY THE TIME I make it back to my apartment. I immediately sneeze as I open the door. *Fucking cat.* The lights are off, and I don't hear Leah. *Maybe she's in bed?* I check my phone. It's still early; she has to be here.

I check her room. The bed's made and Crouton is curled up in a ball on top of it, purring. There's a sick feeling growing in the pit of my stomach. She has no car. Barely any cash. No phone. Nothing. Where the hell could she be?

I walk to the kitchen and flip the light switch.

There's blood on the counter and Leah's nowhere to be found.

Chapter Eight
Leah

I don't know how long I've been sitting here staring at the knife in front of me. My legs ache, feel shaky. I know I shouldn't cut; it's only a temporary release. But I don't know how else to deal with this. Why would Luke drop something like this on my lap and then leave? What did he expect?

I look over to the journal still laying on the kitchen table. I haven't read another word. I'm afraid of what else it might hold, how I might react. I tell myself they're just words; they have no power.

But it's bullshit. Words have power. They can damage you in unseen ways. The wounds may not be noticeable from the outside, but on the inside, they can consume you. It's happening right now. I don't want to believe the words my father wrote in the journal, but deep down I know they're true. I suspected something like this. I just never wanted to believe it could be true.

I grab the knife from the counter with

my right hand and delicately trace my fingertip along the blade's edge. It's sharp—a professional-grade chef's knife. I've never used something this sharp before. When I first started cutting, I was afraid to use anything sharper than the unfolded edge of a paper clip. I didn't want to cut myself too deep.

It sounds weird, but I liked seeing the blood. It was a reminder that I was alive. A living, breathing person—even if my stepmother saw me as worthless.

I began cutting on my thighs, on my hips and upper arms—anywhere that no one would notice. I graduated to safety pins and needles, then razors and utility knives, making deeper cuts the longer I suffered my stepmother's abuse.

The rubber band helps me cope.

I haven't cut in years, but the longer I stare at the cold edge of the blade, the stronger my urge becomes.

I close my eyes and try to control my breathing and calm myself down. *Happy thoughts. Think happy thoughts,* I tell myself. My mind returns to last night, to Luke. I see him again, standing in his room naked. I bite down on my lip as I think about his perfectly sculpted body, about his hands roaming all over mine. My skin tingles, not for release, but for his touch.

We nearly kissed last night. We were inches, moments away from it. I could almost taste his lips. I've always imagined them tasting of mint or cinnamon, something cool or something spicy. But I'm afraid I'll never have the chance. He could have anyone, why would he want me? If he wanted me, he would've kissed me last night when he had the chance. I was begging for it, aching for it, and I know he could feel it too.

But he left. Just like he left years ago. It's what he does. He's reckless with other people's hearts. I need to learn that and move on. But I can't. I'm a stupid, stupid girl with a stupid, stupid crush I'll never get over.

Tears are streaming down my face when I open my eyes and I'm still clutching the knife in my hand. I take my finger and again trace the edge, testing the sharpness one last time. My finger nearly reaches the edge when I hear the front door slam.

My head jerks up and I feel the blade of the knife slice into my fingertip.

"Fuck!" I yell, looking down at my finger. Blood gushes out of the cut and onto my hand and the counter.

I hear a bag drop, then keys, followed by the slow, measured clicking of heels against wood. A tall, slender blonde—model gorgeous—turns the corner and plants her right hand on her hip as she looks at me with her head cocked. The expression on her face says it all: "Who the fuck are you?," "What the fuck are you doing?," and "Am I going to have to call the cops?"

She is wearing a white, expensive looking scoop neck dress with a thin black belt tied around her thin waist; she wears it well and she knows it. I could smell her perfume, bright and citrusy and cheerful. Her bright blue eyes scan me as she bites her lower lip. I know the look. I've seen it time and time again. She's judging me, sizing me up.

Her posture relaxes as she lets her hands fall to her side and her eyes soften. "Are you the new maid?" She turns around to retrieve the bags she left at the door without even waiting for a response.

Maid? Excuse me? A few different thoughts pop into my head. One, Luke didn't tell anyone I was staying here. Two, this person, whoever she was, looked at me once and decided the only reason I would be in Luke's apartment would be to clean it. Three, who the fuck does she think she is? And why does she have a key to Luke's apartment?

When she returns, I tell her I'm Luke's stepsister and that I would be staying here for a few days. I didn't tell her about my stepmother. The last thing I wanted was to hear her spout her insincere platitudes about how sorry she felt for me.

"That's right! I completely forgot Luke had a sister." Her demeanor changes from frigid bitch to best friend. It's amazing how that works, the sudden shift in attitude when a woman no longer sees you as a threat.

"I'm Gretchen, Luke's assistant."

Assistant? I still don't even know what Luke does. Apparently something important if he has his own assistant. Why won't he tell me anything?

She extends her perfectly manicured hand to me. And it's then that I realize I'm still bleeding—a lot—and still gripping the hilt of the knife.

"Oh. My. God." Her olive complexion

washes out, turns ashen as she glimpses the blood on my hand and on the counter tops.

"It was an accident," I say, dropping the knife on the counter. I whip myself around and walk to the sink behind me to wash the blood off my hand. "You surprised me when you walked in." I say cold water runs over my bare skin. "My finger slipped." It *really* was an accident. Honest.

"Just tell me when it's gone." I can hear her feet clicking against the wood floor. "I don't *do* blood." I wasn't aware that people *did* do or *could* do blood. Whatever that means. "Just yell if you need something." Her voice echoes down the hallway.

I watch as the blood circles the drain, mixes with the water, clouds it. *I'm alive,* I tell myself. I dry my hands with a paper towel and toss it in the garbage.

"Hey, Gretchen?" I yell in her general direction.

"Yes?"

"Do you know where the band-aids are?"

"Bathroom. Second drawer down."

She certainly knew her way around this place. It wasn't her first time. I mean, she even had a key. Was she sleeping with

Luke? I could feel my skin flush with jealousy, but I'm able to calm myself. I shouldn't feel jealous—Luke could fuck whoever he wanted (and he always did). I was his stepsister, anyways. And I wasn't his type. She was his type. Tall, skinny, and beautiful. The thought of him ripping off her clothes, his hands running along her naked body made my skin crawl.

I wanted him to do that to me. Not her. Me.

I walk to the bathroom for a band-aid. I can see Gretchen in Luke's room, laying out clothes, putting things away—touching *his* stuff. Why was she touching *his* stuff?

One… two… three… I count in my head. The endorphins from the small cut on my finger have all but dissipated and I'm working myself up again. It seems that every problem in my life revolves around one thing, one person, really: Luke. If I didn't care for him as much as I do, none of this would be bothering me. But I *do* care for him and it *does* bother me when some girl I don't even know rifles through all of his stuff as though they're an item.

Maybe they are…

I don't even want to entertain the idea.

I finish bandaging my cut and walk over to Gretchen. She's neatly folding clothes and placing them in a suitcase on top of Luke's bed.

"What are you doing?" I ask, scrunching my face up.

"Packing." She says blankly, as though it was completely obvious what she was doing and I was stupid for even asking her.

"Why?"

She sighs. "Luke has a photo shoot in New York tomorrow. Didn't you know?"

A Photo shoot? What was she talking about?

"Photo shoot?" My face says it all: I'm lost.

She drops the shirt she's holding on the bed and cocks her head. All that's missing is an eye roll. "Yes. An important one." She sighs. "Honestly, I don't know *how* you couldn't know." She returns to folding. "But I guess… it doesn't *really* surprise me." What the hell was that supposed to mean?

I had only known Gretchen for a few minutes and I knew we would never get along. She was exactly the type of girl I never got along with—a prissy little Barbie. She was one of those fake friends who would befriend me in hopes of getting closer to Luke. Once they finally got what they wanted, or they were rejected, they'd drop me.

She notices me standing in the doorway, brooding, and stops again. "Shouldn't you be packing?"

"Wait, what? Me?"

"Didn't Luke tell you? You're going with him." She said it so matter-of-fact, like this was how it was going to be and there was no other way it could be.

Why would Luke buy me a plane ticket without even telling me, without even knowing that I'd come with him, both here and to New York?

*"*When did you book them? Erhm, the tickets."

"Does it matter?"

"Just curious."

"Hmm… let's see. I'd say a week or two ago." She places the final shirt in the suitcase and zips it up.

Luke had this planned all along, well before he showed up at Buck Wild, well before Judith died. How did he know? How did he know I'd come here, that I'd be left with no other option? Something didn't sit well with me. I didn't like having my life toyed with like this.

"So." Gretchen began, "Do you need any help packing?"

"Uhh… well—" I stammer. I don't have any clothes to pack—I didn't have a chance to grab anything last night. I have nothing but the sweats and t-shirt I'm wearing. Well, I have my cocktail waitress uniform, but I couldn't very well wear that. "I don't have anything with me…" My voice trails off into nothing. A ghost of a voice. I couldn't even look her in the eyes as I talked.

"Don't worry." She says as her eyes rake over me. She cups her chin with her hand, narrows her eyes. "I know exactly what you need."

Chapter Nine
Leah

I HAD NO IDEA what to expect from Gretchen, but I was pleasantly surprised. We went shopping downtown and bought all sorts of elegant and wonderful clothes, clothes that I wouldn't normally wear—not because I didn't like them, but because I couldn't afford them. I didn't pay for a thing. It was all on Luke's dime. My jaw dropped when she whipped out his Black Card.

"Perks of the job." She said with a smile. "He won't mind if I spend a little on his sister."

Later on, we went to a spa: manicures, pedicures, massages, people applying oils and lotions and all sorts of strange things to my body. "We need to treat ourselves," Gretchen said. "Spending all this money is exhausting." We both laughed.

Spas, shopping, makeovers—these weren't things that I'd normally do. I had neither the money nor the time. And I always felt uncomfortable around the type of people who could afford such luxuries, people like Gretchen.

Strangely though, I actually enjoyed it. I enjoyed being attended to, waited on, made to feel special—that I was a person of importance. I had never felt like that once in my life. Although I know Gretchen only did this for me because Luke was her boss, it made me feel a bit better after such a miserable few days, a miserable life, really.

I don't know what would've happened if Gretchen hadn't walked in on me. I certainly wouldn't be standing here outside the door to Luke's apartment with a brand new wardrobe, new hair, and fresh confidence. I might still be in the kitchen, depressed and alone. Or worse yet, laying face down on the floor after cutting too deep. I'm probably exaggerating though.

Anyway, I don't want to think about what could've happened. I want to focus on what did happen. That's what matters.

"I had so much fun today, Gretchen. Thank you." I meant it too. I hadn't once thought about Luke or had the inclination to cut or use my rubber band for release. It was a good day, a first, and it made me forget all about what my dad had written in his journal. At least, for a little while; I'll never completely forget something like that, something that fucked up and twisted and how it affected me.

"Now don't get all warm and fuzzy on me." She says as she turns the key in the lock; pushes open the door. "I guess it was fun, huh? And you look so, so good in that new dress."

I blush. I thought the dress was a bit too revealing, something I wouldn't normally wear. But when I saw the look on Gretchen's face after I walked out of the dressing room —I knew I had to have it. I wanted to see if Luke would have the same response.

The lights are on when we open the door to Luke's apartment. We drop our bags at the door and walk into the main living area, chatting away about nothing in particular. Luke is sitting at the kitchen table, his hands clasped in front of him. He doesn't look happy.

"Gretchen, can I have a word?" He says, calmly, but with enough ice to chill anyone to the bone.

"Uhh… Yeah. Sure." Her voice wavers, laced with uncertainty and apprehension.

Although I've only known Gretchen for a few hours, I've never heard her talk this meekly. I could barely hear her voice and she was standing right next to me.

Luke walks by me as though I'm invisible. His scent flares my nostrils and I breathe it in. Gretchen turns to follow him. I remain still but watch them although I know it's none of my business. I can't make out what they're saying but from what I can see of Gretchen's face, it's not good.

Color drains from her face as Luke talks with her. She hangs her head, averting her gaze from his, letting he arms fall limply to her side. I don't like seeing her being scolded, but I can help but find some satisfaction in knowing she can't be his girlfriend. Luke wouldn't be talking to her like this is she was, right?

She reaches to grab his arm, but he shakes it away. I can see tears stream down her face. She tilts her head towards me, looks at me with tear-filled eyes, and I immediately turn around and walk out of sight. I shouldn't be spying on them.

I mill around in the kitchen, looking for something to drink. I spot the blood on the kitchen counter. *Shit. I completely forgot to clean it up.* I grab a towel, wet it, then wipe away what I can. I don't know where any of his cleaning supplies are, so it's the best I can do at the moment.

I feel Crouton rub his face against my leg and meow. "Oh my god, Crouton! I completely forgot to feed you before I left." I'm just not with it today. Or most days, for that matter.

I pick him up and creep to my bedroom, trying to be as inconspicuous as possible. Leah and Gretchen are still talking and I don't want to disturb them any more than I already have. I find Crouton's bowl—it's full. *Luke actually fed him?* I'm a little stunned. I thought he hated cats—Crouton especially. Maybe I'm wrong about Luke.

That thought was quickly shot down when Luke bursts into my room not much later.

"What the fuck were you thinking?" He demands.

I don't know how to respond. I can feel my stomach turn, my body grow cold. There was a fierceness in his eyes, rage running through him like a wildfire, and I was the target.

"Jesus, Leah," He sighs, his eyes

softening. He sits down on my bed and stares at me. "You scared the shit out of me." He runs his right hand through his hair. I should probably say something, but I can't. I'm frozen in place.

"I come home to find that not only were you gone, but there was blood all over the countertop." He stares at me with his pale blue eyes, and I can sense a sort of sadness in them, or is it disappointment? "I mean, what the fuck?"

I had never seen this side of him, caring and concerned. I never knew it *could* exist in him. He was always tough, stoic even, and there wasn't a time that I could remember where he showed even an ounce of emotion. Not once. It was throwing me off, but I found myself even more attracted to him because of it.

I walk over to him slowly, sit down next to him. I want to tell him the truth, but was afraid he'd be disgusted with me, think I was some freak for wanting to cut myself. So I do what anyone else in my position would do. I lie.

"I'm sorry," I tell him. "I was making lunch and cut myself. Gretchen dropped in shortly after that and I got distracted; I forgot to clean up the blood. Then we left to go shopping." He's staring blankly at the wall in front of him.

I feel self-conscious, ashamed of myself for lying; I was never good at it.

But then I remember. I remember why I shouldn't be the one feeling embarrassed, why I shouldn't be defensive. What did it matter if I forgot to clean up the blood or left without writing a note? He was the one who dropped in out of nowhere and expected me to drop everything for him, follow him without question. He dropped the fucking bombshell that is my father's journal without so much as an explanation.

If anyone should be angry, it should be me.

"So when were you going to tell me you booked me a ticket to New York with you? *Weeks* ago I might add. How the hell did you know I'd even come with you? And would you care to explain what the hell I read in my dad's journal?"

"You seem angry." He turns his head and smiles at me. That cocky, shit-eating grin. That's the Luke I'm used to, condescending, uncaring—a fucking asshole.

I want to scream. It was always so

infuriating dealing with him. I can feel myself flush.

"Fucking. Asshole." The words come from somewhere deep. I almost don't even recognize my own voice.

"Whoa, whoa, whoa. Take it easy." He says, placing a hand on my shoulder which I immediately shrug off; the weight and feel of his hand linger on my shoulder and my skin tingles. Even though I can't stand him right now, I still want him to touch me, feel his hands all over my body. It's sick; it's twisted; I know. I can't help it.

His face tells me he's amused. He enjoys toying with me, seeing me get frustrated, working me up into a frenzy.

"If I don't get answers, I'm going to walk out that door," I say more calmly.

"And go where, exactly?" He says as he raises his eyebrows. His scent is beginning to overwhelm me, making my thoughts muddled and my heart race. He knew my words were hollow; I had nowhere to go and even if I did, I wouldn't act.

But I knew what would rile him up. Two could play this game.

"I'll take Miles up on his offer." His body tenses up at the sound of his name.

"No. You won't." Luke growls. It catches me off guard—his voice. It's rough and fierce and makes my hair stand on end. I almost regret saying it. "You're going to stay here with me."

"Well, aren't you demanding."

"And you're sexy when you're mad." Electricity surges through me; I feel light-headed. I brace myself on the bed so I don't fall backward. No one had called me sexy before, and I had never thought of myself as sexy. Not in the slightest. This coming from Luke—it had to be another game, some misdirection to throw me off. He couldn't mean it. Could he?

I search his eyes, study his face; I'm trying to figure out if this is some game or not.

"It's true." He says as though he can read my mind. "You're sexy when you're not mad too." His eyes rake over me. My skin burns under his gaze.

This can't be real. This can't be happening. This was never supposed to happen.

"Did Gretchen pick out this outfit?" I was wearing a white V-neck dress that was almost as revealing as my uniform. It's the first dress that fits me well, accentuates my curves. And, to be honest, I did feel sexy in it. There's a first time for everything.

I can feel myself flush as Luke shifts closer to me. I can feel his breath on me cheek. I pull at the hem of the dress, try to readjust to show less leg.

Luke grabs my wrist hard. "What are you doing?" I recognize the look in his eyes: Lust. He wants me. It's the same look he had last night. My skin burns under his grip and my heart beats out of my chest.

"I was just—" I don't have the chance to finish. I let out a gasp as he slides his hand along me thigh, pushes my dress up, revealing a milky white thigh. If he goes any further, he may be able to see some of my scars. I want him to. I want to reveal myself completely to him.

"That's better." His sultry voice wraps around me like velvet.

He places his hand on mine while the other traces shapes across my thigh. "What are you doing to me, Leah?"

I don't know how to respond.

"What... What do you mean?"

He looks at me, lust flooding through his pale blue eyes, then snatches my wrists before I have the chance to react and forcefully pins me against the bed. I struggle, but only a little—it's turning me on far more than it should, more than I'm letting on.

"You make me want to do things." He rasps as he straddles me. "Things I shouldn't do." The light smell of his cologne mixes with his natural scent and creates a heady musk that I can't get enough of; it envelopes me completely and I can feel my inhibitions melt away.

I writhe under him as his fingers trace a line along my cheek, down my neck and across my chest. His right hand pins my wrists above my head. My body is on fire at the thought of what he'll do next, all the things he could next.

He leans in close, his lips nearing the bare skin of my neck but not touching it; a flip of his hair tickles my cheek. My skin tingles and burns and aches for the sweet touch of his lips.

"What… what are you doing?" I ask.

"Finishing what I started last night." He tells me, his breath tickling my neck.

"We can't, Luke. It's wrong." I say, my words betraying my true feelings. I want him. I have for as long as I can remember. If this was wrong, why did it feel so right? I don't care about what happened in the past; all I care about is what was happening now, between us.

"I'll decide what's wrong." He snarls.

Desire and lust and every fantasy I've had about Luke floods through me, but fear rises to the surface from somewhere deep inside me. I fear that he'll leave again, that I'll give him what he wants and he'll cast me aside like every other girl. I don't want that to happen. I don't want to be like every other girl. I *won't* be like every other girl.

"No," I say, more forcefully this time. "No, we can't do this." I try to break free from his grasp, but he's too strong.

But then he relents. "Fine." He says coldly, his voice devoid of any emotion. He pulls away, lets go of my wrists. "If you want to stop we can stop." My heart sinks into my stomach. I feel sick and I instantly regret everything I just said. He keeps looking at me, scanning my face for something.

"Do you want to stop?" He asks.

I don't, but I'm at a crossroads. My mind tells me to follow the path to the right: end it now before you get hurt. But my heart and everything else tells me to follow the left path: give in—it's what you've always wanted.

I don't want him to leave, so I say nothing, hoping he will do what I don't want to vocalize. *Fuck me.* I lay there, looking up at his handsome face as his eyes rake across my body. I feel naked under his gaze.

He grins—a devilish and cocky grin, a knowing grin. He knows what I want. And he knows I'm afraid to say it.

He leans in again, his hands sliding along my bare arms, forcing them back over my head. His lips are centimeters away from mine. I can almost taste them. I want to taste him. I bit down hard on my lower lip as I writhe under the weight of his body. I can feel his hard cock under his clothes, pushing against me.

"I didn't think so." He rasps.

I gasp as his lips touch my skin just below my ear. Goosebumps erupt along my neck, along my arms and legs. It was only a kiss, but my body was on fire, aching for more. He kisses my jaw, continues lower along my neck, his stubble scratching my sensitive skin.

He tears at the straps on my shoulder, revealing my bare breasts.

"Fucking hell, Leah." He growls. "You're gorgeous. Fucking sexy." Gorgeous. Sexy. Those were words used to describe other women—not me. But he meant it. I could see it in his eyes, hear it in his voice.

"You're mine." He tells me. "Say it."

"I'm yours," I whisper.

"Louder!" He snarls.

"I'm yours," I repeat, but with more conviction.

He's laid his claim, stuck a flag in me. I'm his. And I like that. I like the idea of being his, something to be claimed. My core floods with desire. I want to feel him inside me. I want him to fuck me and fuck me properly, finish what he started.

"That's it." He says. "And you'll do as I say."

"Yes. I will." I moan, grinding myself against him. "Fuck me, Luke. Just fuck me." I beg. I can feel myself getting more and more wet. I've worked myself into a frenzy and I need release.

"Is that what you want? You want me to fuck that tight little pussy of yours?"

"Yes, Luke. Please. Please fuck me."

"Strip." He demands, pulling away from me, allowing me to move more freely.

I take off my dress; I'm only wearing panties. But not for long.

"God damn, Leah. Your body is amazing." He runs his hands along my bare skin, along my thighs. His thumbs graze my pussy as he rubs me, forcing me to moan softly. He rips my panties to the side—my wet center exposed—and slides a finger inside.

"Oh fuck, Luke." I gasp.

"You're so wet, Leah."

I grind against him as his fingers slide in and out, in and out of my wet hole, repeatedly, and with no end in sight. I'm nearing climax, my orgasm welling deep inside me—I'm moments away.

"Like that…" I moan. "Just like that. I'm about to—"

But then he stops. He pulls his fingers out of me and stands up.

"Wha.. What?" I mutter.

"Go to bed." He says, coldly. "Don't ever leave again without telling me.

"Fuck you!" I scream at him, but it's no use, he's already shut the door behind him.

What the fuck was his problem? What

exactly was his deal? How could he just switch everything off like that?

You should've seen it coming, the more logical part of me tells me. *He's always been like this. He likes to control people. He gets off on it.*

I slam my fists against the bed. How could I be so stupid? Luke never wanted me. He was toying with me the entire time. I fall back against my pillows; Crouton hops on my bed, cuddling next to me. "You're the only one I can trust, Crouton," I whisper, stroking his soft fur as her purrs. "I can't even trust myself."

I toss and turn in bed for a while, frustrated, but eventually fall asleep.

CHAPTER TEN
LEAH

IN MY DREAM, I see Judith. I'm laying in bed and she's sitting next to me, dabbing my forehead with a washcloth. "I hate seeing my baby sick." She tells me in a soothing voice. There's an ethereal glow around her, and something about her demeanor unsettles me.

I try to speak; I open my mouth, but nothing comes out. My voice is gone. My throat is tight. I can't even move. Fear floods through me.

She's wearing a white nightgown. Wisps of her light brown hair fall over he pallid skin. Her thin lips are closed tight in a ghost of a smile—or is it sneer?

"Here." She says. "Drink this." She takes a mug from the nightstand, swirls the liquid with a spoon, metal clinking against ceramic, and offers it to me. I close my lips tightly, shake my head, like a child refusing to eat mushed food. "Now, Leah. No one likes a brat. Obey your mother." She tries to force my mouth open with the spoon, but still I resist.

"Just a sip." She coos. "I promise you'll feel much better."

My mouth opens wide on its own accord. I can't close it. "That's it." She places the spoon on the nightstand and turns back to me. "That's a good girl." She pours the liquid into my mouth, tipping the mug so a steady stream of disgusting and bitter liquid begins to fill my mouth. It becomes thick and syrupy and impossible to swallow.

I can't breathe. I'm choking and coughing and crying and my body is convulsing wildly.

I wake up to Luke shaking me.

"Leah… Hey, Leah—it's okay." He pulls me into him and I fold into his body. I can feel warm tears stream down my cheeks. "You're okay. I'm here." His embrace is warm and comforting and for a moment I forget about my dream.

"I… I…" I whimper. I can't think, can't formulate any coherent thought.

"Shhh… Don't speak." He strokes my hair. It's comforting, his touch, and eventually I calm down. It was only a dream. It didn't mean anything. It didn't mean anything… I repeat in my head over and over again.

"Lay down," Luke whispers into my ear. "Just lay down and relax. I'll be here until you fall asleep."

"No," I beg. "Stay with me. Please."

He looks at me, then nods. "Okay."

It was then that I notice he isn't wearing a shirt and neither was I. I was so frustrated with him that I didn't even think about dressing for bed—I just fell asleep.

I roll over onto my side, trying to force images of Luke's chiseled abs, his perfect body, out of my mind. It was hopeless though. With Luke laying down next to me, it was all I could think about.

His body radiates heat and I feel his arm reach over my side and latch itself onto me. It's warm and smooth and more muscled than I remember. I try to pull away, but he pulls me closer. I can feel his hard cock push against my ass.

"Where are you going?" His tone is soft, playful even. He grabs my breast and moan escapes me.

"Luke," I breathe, "Luke, stop it. Please. Stop toying with me."

"Is that what you think I'm doing?" He

asks bluntly.

I flip over on my other side so I can face him. I get lost for a moment as my eyes wander over his broad shoulders, strong chest, and perfect v taper. I shake myself out of it and refocus.

"It's exactly what you're doing," I say, trying to be stern, but it didn't come across that way as all he did was shoot me a cocky smile.

He reaches out and cups my breasts, massages them in his strong hands. Pleasure erupts throughout my body. My nipples harden under his fingers.

I hate how even after all that he had put me through, continues to put me through, I can't stay mad at him no matter how hard I try. He's gorgeous and perfect and everything I want. I hate it. I hate myself for falling for him this hard.

"No!" I yell. "Stop it! I've had enough." He stops.

"Fine." He says brusquely. "Have it your way."

He gets up and leaves and I'm left alone in bed, wondering if I ruined my chances with him.

CHAPTER ELEVEN
LUKE

I MAY HAVE PUSHED Leah too far. There's a thin line between confidence and arrogance, and I crossed it. I pushed when I should've pulled. Normally, I wouldn't care. I could have anyone I wanted.

Leah's different though, different from all the other girls I've had. She actually means something to me. I realized that the moment I saw the blood on the counter and she was gone. But I guess I knew it much earlier than that, the night I was forced to leave her, years ago.

It's strange for me to even think this way. I never let anyone get this close, never let anyone in. I use people, take what I want from them, and discard them like trash when I'm done. It's a cruel world, and I'm no saint.

Leah's the first person who might change that, but I'm pushing her away. It's probably for the best.

This isn't supposed to happen.

I'm not supposed to fall for Leah.

It can only end in pain—there is no other way.

Leah has been moody all morning, and rightly so. I was an asshole last night. She's picking at her eggs and hasn't eaten anything yet. She hasn't spoken once. What's going on in her mind? What is she thinking about? Normally, I wouldn't ask these questions, but for once I'm genuinely interested.

She drops her fork; it clanks against the plate.

She looks at me but doesn't say a word; she doesn't have to, anyway—her face says it all. I smile, but it seems to irritate her more. Oops.

Finally, she speaks: "Did they find out how Judith died?"

"If they did, they're keeping it a secret." I take a drink of my coffee. It tastes more bitter than usual.

"Why were you at mom's house the day she died? Why did you show up out of the blue?" She's staring at me now with those watery, green eyes—large and round. She has kind, beautiful face, and I want to kiss it.

Why did she have to ask me that?

I clear my throat, grab a pill from my pocket, and pop it in my mouth. I take a large gulp of water and swallow it. We were about to leave for New York. This wasn't something I could explain in five minutes. But the way she regarded me, behind those stray strands of chestnut hair, I could tell that I was on thin ice. And she wasn't about to let me off the hook.

"You read Robert's journal, right?" I lay my hands, palm down, on the table. She turns her head away, looks at the floor. I can see the color drain from her face. She shuts her eyes. When she looks at me again, her eyes are filled with tears.

"Some of it." I can barely hear her; her voice is weak and trembling, laced with sadness and pain and uncertainty. She has an idea, but she doesn't know the whole story.

"Are you sure you want to hear everything right now?" I ask.

I watch as she snaps the rubber band around her wrist against her skin. She does this a few times before letting out a sigh. Why does she keep on doing it? What purpose does it serve? I've been trying to figure it out ever since I picked her up that night.

"Yes." She says, her cheeks stained with tears, her eyes puffy. "I want to know."

I rub my eyes as pressure builds in my head; my vision blurs once I stop. It takes a few moments for my eyes to readjust, but when they do, Leah's beautiful face comes into focus and I almost forget what we were talking about. I'm lost in her eyes, the way the morning sun strikes her left cheek, her cherry lips. She's innocent and pure and I'm no good for her.

"No questions. Not until I finish."

"I understand." She takes a deep breath then exhales silently.

"Everything I'm about to tell you, I did it for you. Remember that."

She sits there, her head slightly bowed but still looking at me.

I run a hand through my hair, take a deep breath, and begin my story, starting with the night I left, the night when everything I thought I knew about my life unraveled—the night it all began.

Part Three

Chapter Twelve
Luke

"When I said goodbye to you that night, I had no idea it would be years until I saw you again." Leah shifts in her chair and places her forearms on the edge of the table. She pulls the sleeves of her sweatshirt over her hands so only her fingertips peek out.

I see movement in my periphery. Crouton's creeping out of Leah's room and slinking over to us. So much for our agreement. Whatever.

I clear my throat. "I left for my date with Marissa. We were heading to—"

"Save it." Leah snaps at me as her eyes harden under knit eyebrows. "You were going to fuck her. I get it. Fast forward to the part where you skipped out on me." She crosses her arms over her chest as she leans back in her chair and stares blankly at the floor beside her.

"Have it your way." I say calmly as I clasp my hands in front of me. "After I *fucked* Marissa..." I let the words hang in the air for a moment before continuing. "We had an argument. I ended up coming home earlier than expected. Mom was in the kitchen."

I take a moment—close my eyes and breathe in deeply. The smell of the bacon I made for breakfast still lingers in the air. I let the breath out softly, slowly. When I open my eyes again, Leah's staring at me. It's almost unnerving how intense her gaze is. Her face and eyes are still red and puffy from the tears, and her hair is tied up in a messy bun; even so, she's still gorgeous. And for a moment, I'm caught up in her beauty.

"I was a little tipsy when I came back, so I wasn't sure if I was imagining what I was seeing. She had all these bottles and pills and vials and I don't know what else scattered across the kitchen table."

A sick feeling begins to well up in my stomach. There isn't much that phases me, but rehashing buried secrets is one of them.

I should've put an end to it then. I should've gone upstairs, pulled her out of bed and left, never to look back.

But I didn't. I was a kid back then. My only priorities were getting drunk and fucking. I wasn't prepared for shit like this. No one is.

"Well, I kept my distance as I watched her. I watched as she transferred powders and strange liquids to the soup that was cooking on the stove. I'll never forget the creepy grin she had plastered on her face. The way her thin lips closed tightly together as they stretched into an even thinner smile. There was this wild look to her. Her face had always been pale, but it seemed to glow. Stray hairs fell across her face and the silver locket around her neck swung as she walked back and forth, stirring the soup, adding powders, but never tasting." My fist strikes the table hard, shaking it and sending Crouton sprinting out from under it and down the hall. "She never tasted anything. It never struck me as odd until that moment, watching her as she prepared your soup."

I hear Leah sniffle, then watch as she wipes her tears away with the back of her sleeve. She looks up at me with her sad face and her sad wet eyes and I know she knows, but she's waiting for me to say the words. Maybe there's a chance it's all some elaborate joke? A sick and twisted joke, but a joke nonetheless. I wish. But there's no punch line at the end.

"I don't know how much of the journal you've read, but if you read much of it, you already know what I'm getting at."

"Say it." She says. Her voice is brittle and weak, almost unrecognizable. If there were a breeze, it would carry it off before it had the chance to cross the few feet that separate us.

"Judith has been poisoning you."

"And you're certain about this?" She asks. Her eyes go glassy and she wrings her hands in front of her. There's no color in her face, except for her lips. It's as though all the color from her face has pooled into those rosy red lips. I want to kiss them again, taste their sweetness, but now isn't the time.

I nod. "Yes."

"How do you know?"

She doesn't want to believe it, and I don't blame her. How could someone do something this fucked up? And for what reason? I've asked myself these questions and more many times before, but it doesn't make sense no matter how I look at it. I wish I could tell her there's a chance that I'm wrong, that my mother wasn't poisoning her, that it was only a coincidence she became sick when she moved in with us.

It's not.

It's the truth.

I've spent so much time piecing it all together. All the way back to my real father.

"When I was 10 years old, we moved to Milton—into the house we lived in together." He motions between us. "It was a few years before my mother met your father. My real father, Dan, was still alive." I let out a strained sigh. "Judith hated everything about Milton. She hated being dragged there. She resented my father for taking a job there. She wasn't happy and she made it abundantly clear." I study Leah's face as I take another sip of water. Her face is blank, devoid of any emotion. She's just sitting there, watching me with empty eyes.

"My father started getting sick, much like how you were." I nod at her. "It started with headaches, upset stomachs, and then grew into something much worse. Some days he could barely get out of bed." I look down as I run a hand through my hair, then look back up at Leah. "For a 10-year-old boy, seeing your father—someone who seems invincible—unable to get out of bed fucks with your head." I've never told anyone this. I've kept it buried, deep inside me for so many years. "No one knew what was wrong. No doctor could help him. He just kept getting worse until he died—cardiac arrest. Just like Robert."

I could feel myself heating up.

"She took my father's life; she took my stepfather's life; she nearly took yours." My voice was shaking with rage and I slam my fist on the table again; the water glass tips over, and plates and silverware clink together.

"And there was nothing I could do about it. I was powerless. I had no control. When I confronted her that night—the night that I left—she denied poisoning you. She denied everything. She told me I was crazy, making things up. That everything she was doing was for your sake. To help you. She believed that. Even up until the day she died." I shake my head. "Things got out of hand and Robert ended up throwing me out. I tried to tell him the truth—warn him—but he didn't believe me. Why would he? All he could see was a mother trying to help her ailing stepdaughter and an eighteen-year-old who was violent and out of control. He told me I had to leave; I wasn't welcome anymore."

"So I left," I say, shrugging. "I had no other options. I was eighteen. Who was going to believe a crazy story like that?"

"You could've taken me with you." She says in almost a whisper.

"Yeah, that would've worked. Two broke teenagers. Sounds like a great plan." I spit. I didn't mean for it to come out so harsh, but the anger I felt building just spilled out.

"Seems like it worked out just fine for you." She snaps back. There's a hardness to her eyes, a sharp edge to her voice. She had a point, albeit a small one. She doesn't realize the absolute hell I went through to achieve what I have today, the days when I had no idea if I was going to eat or not. I was lucky—in the right place at the right time. I know this. She doesn't.

"It wasn't as easy as you make it out to be." I sigh. "You were better off staying with Judith and Robert." She shakes her head with disgust as she folds her arms. "He promised me that he'd protect you, keep an eye out on the off chance that I was telling him the truth. I was trying to help you. Taking you with me would've caused more issues than it fixed."

"Help me?" All the color that had drained from her face earlier is back. "Help me?" She repeats. She peels back the sleeve on her right arm and shoves it toward me. "Look!" Tears fall from her eyes as she yells at me. "Just look at what your help did!"

There's a scar on her forearm, about midway up. It's raised and pink and shaped… like an L? I can't tell. She pulls the sleeve of her sweater back down to cover it. Then she slumps back in her chair.

"I had been cutting for years." She tells me as she looks off to the side. The reality of it hits hard and disorients me. I never knew she cut—I had no idea. But it explains a lot. "Cutting helped me cope with the shit Judith put me through. And when you left, everything got worse. Her nagging, her passive-aggressive bullshit—everything. I decided to cut the reason for my pain into my arm. A reminder. A warning. Your name."

I feel gutted, and for the first time in my life I can't look another person in the eyes. I never realized just how much I meant to her, or how my leaving affected her.

"It was an accident." She adds, her lips quivering as she tries to hold herself together. "I cut too deep and everyone thought I tried to kill myself. I didn't mean for it to happen." Tears are flooding her cheeks now and her voice is rough and cracks as she continues to talk. "I begged and pleaded, but they took me away anyway —'to get me help.'"

There's a stabbing pain in my chest and it's becoming difficult to breath. I take another pill and try to swallow but my throat is so sore and lumpy and tight that I can't. I can't swallow a tiny fucking pill. I cough and sputter as Leah continues to stare at me with wet, helpless eyes. The kind of eyes you see from a stray.

'Help me,' They say. 'Love me.'

I don't know what to say. What can you say in a situation like this? Nothing I could possibly come up could change anything, could comfort or help her. I say the only words I can think of, but as soon as they leave my lips, I know they won't help.

"I'm sorry."

And for the first time in my life, I meant it.

I was sorry for not taking her with me that night.

I was sorry for the pain I caused her

when I left.

I was sorry that I never made it clear to her just how much she meant to me.

I was sorry that I didn't protect her like I should have.

I was… sorry.

But 'sorry' isn't enough to fix scar tissue that deep.

I'M 41,000 FEET IN the air *en route* to New York. The seat next to mine is as empty as the small bottle of scotch in front of me. The only person I've ever cared for—loved, actually—is miles away.

I've never felt this way about someone before.

I've never felt this much remorse.

Luke Hammond has feelings?

Sometimes.

I keep replaying our conversation over in my head. Was there something I could've said differently? Some magical word that would change everything? I don't know.

I told her why I had to leave her years ago, and how I had confronted Judith in order to protect her. I *did* try to protect her.

I told her everything, and I told her the truth. All of it. But it didn't matter: she left anyway.

The only place she hasn't left is my mind.

She's the song I can't get out of my head.

Chapter Thirteen
Leah

July 4th, 2013

It's been a while since I've been able to write. Not because I have nothing to write about, quite the opposite. In fact, almost too much has happened in the past few days that I don't know where to begin. But, I guess I have to start somewhere…

I left Luke after he told me everything. I still don't know if I believe him, but everything he told me about Judith makes sense.

I only became sick when I moved into that house.

I got better when I left.

My father got sick when I left…

I just don't want to believe that people like her exist in this world.

That I lived with her for so long without knowing…

That Luke knew about it and didn't tell me.

Didn't save me.

He tried to stop me from leaving, but I wouldn't budge. I needed time alone. Time to think about everything.

I shouldn't have been so hard on him. He couldn't have saved me. I know that now. He was a kid and so was I.

Even if he tried to take me away that night, my Judith would be crazy enough to tell the police he kidnapped me after assaulting her. It would be a bullshit sob story, but she'd be convincing. Fake tears and self-inflicted bruises.

I wouldn't put it past her. Not anymore.

And I can't blame Luke for what happened to me. I can't blame anyone else but myself for being sent to Millwood. I was a teenager, prone to theatrics. I made a mistake, and I paid the price.

I probably should have told him that, but I didn't. I was still so angry with him, with everything he told me.

You can't ask someone to think rationally after something like that. Oh well.

Even though I was sent to Millwood for a misunderstanding, I see it now as a blessing in disguise. It got me out of the house and away from Judith. I learned other ways to cope and I even started to paint again. It actually wasn't that bad, now that I think about it. It was a breeze compared to living with Judith.

It feels good to get everything out. I've held everything in for so long that I feel as though my insides have twisted themselves into one tangled knot.

Slowly, I feel that knot unraveling. The more I use this journal, the smaller that knot becomes.

I haven't used my rubber band in days. That's a first. It's like I'm throwing away my crutches. I can finally begin to walk again.

Even after the news about Judith, I think things will be better.

How could they get any worse?

I'm meeting with Miles in a few hours. He wants to talk to me about Luke.

I'm hesitant, but I decided to go one one condition: That he returns Judith's Locket.

I want to destroy something she loved.

Petty, I know. But after what she put me through, I think I can get away with a little pettiness.

Just this once.

IT'S ONLY A TEN-MINUTE walk from my

house to the dive bar I'm meeting Miles at. 25 if you're walking at my pace.

I don't really want to do this. I don't want to talk about Luke, or hear what Miles has to say about him. But, I have no other choice. I either meet with him now or I meet with him later when he calls me into the station. Either way we're going to meet.

I just want it to be on neutral ground.

I picked this bar for no other reason than that I could walk to it. I'd never actually been inside because I don't normally frequent bars. Especially ones like this.

The exterior has seen better days. Maybe. Probably not. Neon signs litter windows. Coors. Miller. Bud. The usual suspects. I've never had the taste for beer. I've tried it, but I've just never liked it. Too bitter. Too… It's disgusting. That's all.

I'm a few feet away from the metal door. A large bouncer leans against the building with his back and one foot as his fingers nimbly type texts. He doesn't bother to check my I.D. He just grunts and waves me by like he's shooing away an annoying kid as he continues to type away.

This place isn't exactly hopping.

The interior is about what you'd expect

from the outside. A tattooed barman with stringy black hair, a goatee, and a long, hooked nose chats with the only customer seated at the bar. An old man. A regular, I'd guess. The smell he emits as I pass by tells me that he hasn't showered in days. If he showers at all.

The floor sticks to my shoes as I walk, gummy with spilt beer and who knows what else.

Miles is seated at a booth in the back. He waves me over with a smile and I weave through a couple of pool tables on my way. A man wearing a dark hoody bumps into me hard as I try to walk by him.

"What the fuck?"He just shrugs his shoulder and sits down at a table a few feet away. Some people.

A wave of nerves crashes over me as I sit down.

"I'm glad you could make it. Sorry about —" He nods to the guy I just bumped into. His face is shadowed by his hood, but I can see his mouth curve into snarl before he takes a sip of his drink. There's something oddly familiar about him, and I get the sense that he's watching me.

"It's fine." I say, shaking it off.

Miles beams at me. His green eyes seem to shimmer in the dim lit. I won't fall for them again.

"So," he begins. "First things first." He clasps his hand in front of him.

"The locket."

"About that." He tilts his head as he looks down at the table, then back up to me. "There was no locket."

"Wait, what?"

I don't understand. It was a keepsake from her mother and she never took it off. Not in the shower, not for bed, not even for me. I remember asking her once—and only once—if I could hold it. Not even wear it. She smiled at me as though I just asked her the most ridiculous question. "Maybe when you're older, dear." She patted my head and then walked away.

I hated that locket. She loved it more than me. A stupid piece of metal and I wanted to throw it in a river and watch it float away, never to be seen again.

But, if it really is gone, what does it matter?

"She wasn't wearing a locket when we found her."

I shrug my shoulders and begin to get

up. Miles places his hand on mine. "Just a few minutes. It's all I'm asking for."

I exhale loudly through my nose, look at him for a long moment, but sit back down.

"Thanks."

His hand is still on mine. My skin begins to tingle. I tear it out from under his and fold my hands on my lap.

"What do you know about the night Judith was murdered?"

"Murdered?" I blurt.

My mouth hangs open. It never crossed my mind. Why would anyone…

It doesn't make sense.

No. It couldn't be Luke. Luke would never do something like that. Just because he was the last person—last known person—to see her alive doesn't mean he killed her.

He told me what happened, and I believe him.

"I'm sorry, Leah. I'm afraid it's true."

I look down and see that I'm twisting knots in my shirt.

"Look." His voice jolts my attention back to him. "I asked you here because I need your help. We have a few leads, but we don't have all the information. I was hoping you could tie up a few loose ends."

My eyes are drawn back to the man I bumped into, sitting only a few tables away from us. I swear he's staring at me, but I can't see his eyes. His long fingers are wrapped around a small, stout glass with amber liquid in it. It's beginning to creep me out.

"Fine." I say, picking at my nails. "What do you want to know?"

"Has Luke mentioned why he was at his mother's house?"

"To save me." I blurt out without even thinking.

"To save you? What do you mean?"

He folds his arms across his chest as he looks at me with a furrowed brow.

Why was he confused? How could he not know after talking to Luke? Did Luke not tell him? How could he not? Something wasn't adding up.

"He found out that she was poisoning me. Making me sick."

"Uh huh." He nods. "And how did he know this?"

I tell him the story—all of it—from the beginning, all the way up to the last moment when Judith attacked Luke. His face isn't telling me anything. It's… impassive.

As I was telling the story, I could feel myself doubting it. There was no physical proof except for my father's journal and the fact that I kept getting sick when I was back at home. How did I know the food I was eating making me sick?

It was the first question he asked me, and all I could say was: "I don't know. I was almost always sick when I was there. You know that. It wasn't every day, but it was often enough. I stopped getting sick when I left…" I rub my scar underneath the table. "For Millwood. And when I came home… sick again."

Miles rubs his chin, considering what I just told him.

"Okay." That's all he said. A single, 'okay.'

I look back to where the hooded man was seated, but he's gone.

"Don't you find it odd that Luke discovers this… this secret about your mother. About her harming you. And that she ends up dead the night he comes back?"

Yes. Wait, no. I don't know. I know it seems odd, but I know Luke didn't kill Judith. He's not…

"He didn't kill Judith." I make sure to keep my voice calm but assertive.

Miles shakes his head. "I'm not saying that—"

"But you're implying it!" I snap back. Oops.

"Leah. I go where the evidence takes me. And right now it's pointing me right to Luke."

"What evidence? All you know is that he was *supposedly* the last person to see her alive. Luke would never—"

I can feel myself choking up. I hate this. I hate Miles for making me doubt Luke.

"What do you really know about Luke?"

What do I know about him? I know he didn't kill anyone. But it doesn't matter. Miles will paint his own picture no matter what I say.

"I'll tell you what I know." He says, pointing at himself, his eyes wide. "I know he's intelligent, manipulative, and an excellent liar. He lied about his story at the station. I know that now after the story you told me. He said Judith attacked him because he wouldn't give her money. Not because he wanted to take you away."

Why would he lie about that? I don't get

it. I'm tired of listening. I just want to leave.

"He's not who you think he is, Leah."

"No, Miles." I tell him, sternly, as I stand up to leave. " He's not who *you* think he is."

He grabs my arm just before I reach the door. He tells me to listen and whispers into my ear what they found in Luke's car—the pills he had in the glove compartment. They showed up in Judith's toxicology report. I try to explain to him that Luke needs those pills for his congenital heart defect. And that he should know that, too. He's been taking those pills since he was a kid.

I couldn't explain why they were in Judith's report, but they wouldn't have killed her. Miles agrees, but he tells me that the other drugs they found would. And that there was already a team at Luke's apartment searching for them.

I rip myself from his grasp and walk away, disappearing around the corner as Miles watches me from the doorway.

I don't want to think about it any longer.

I CAN'T SHAKE THE feeling that I'm being followed.

But every time I look my shoulder, I don't see anyone. I'm the only person on the street. It's quiet. The only noise comes from the slight breeze rustling the leaves of the sycamores that line the street. The breeze brings with it the smell of rain.

He's manipulative, and an excellent liar. He's not who you think he is.

It couldn't be true, could it? Why would Luke kill his mother? He had no motive, no reason to do it. Well, other than the fact that she was poisoning me. But that wouldn't be enough to make him kill his mother, right?

Six minutes. That's how long it takes me to get back.

Ugh. I stick out my jaw and blow a stray tendril of hair off my face as I fish out the house key from my purse. It doesn't work— the blowing. The hair just falls right back in place.

The door clicks open just as I hear rapid footfall behind me—the swish of feet against grass, across the cement path leading to the house, then onto the wood steps and porch. I'm too slow to react. Two arms wrap themselves around me, lift me off the floor as I struggle and take me inside.

A filthy hand with long and even filthier fingers reaches up and stifles my screams.

"Well, what have we got here." I smell

his breath before I hear his words. It's sweet with alcohol but putrid. I can picture the slimy yellow teeth peeking through his snarl.

I don't have to see his face to know It's Gabe. I know his voice just as well as his stench.

I try to scream; my legs flail wildly as he carries me over to the sofa in the living room.

"Squeal for me. Squeal like the goddamned whore you are. I don't mind one bit. Gonna make it more fun. Keep it up."

The more he talks, the more I feel like gagging. He smells as though he hasn't showered for weeks, months even. His teeth have probably never seen a toothbrush.

Our bodies crash against the sofa and his arms are still wrapped tightly around me. The weight of him against me is enough to knock the breath out of me and force my mouth open and gasp for air. Small, dirty breaths of air, filtered through Gabe's fingers, fill my lungs.

I feel like giving up. No matter where I go or what I do, nothing ever turns out right. What's the point in trying?

No! I tell myself. *Fight back!*

His hand slides away from my mouth and I can breathe clean air again.

"Please, Gabe." I pant. "Please don't hurt me."

He moves back onto his knees and forcibly turns me over onto my back. Taking my wrists in his hands, he pins me against the couch. We're face to face, only a few inches between us. He's wearing the same hoody as the man I saw in the corner of the bar. It was him.

He's been watching me, stalking me.

I feel sick.

"Oh, I ain't gonna hurt ya." He snarls. A wild glint flickers in his eyes. They're open so wide they're almost all white. "We're gonna have ourself a little fun. A good ole time." He lets go of my wrists to unbuckle his belt.

This is my opening, my only chance. I can't count on anyone else to get me out of this situation. It probably won't work—I've never punched anyone before—but what other options do I have?

Crotch or gut?

I only have a split-second to decide: Crotch.

My punch connects and judging by the

howl coming from him; it works. He topples over to the side, and I'm able to free myself. I'm on my feet; I scurry around the coffee table and head for the door. His hand shoots toward my leg as I pass by, and he snags my ankle.

"You ain't going nowhere, you fucking bitch." He growls.

I'm balancing myself on one leg as I try to kick his grip away with the other. But it's not enough. He has already recovered from whatever damage my punch inflicted and a second hand snags my other leg. With one effortless pull, I fall flat on my face.

"Please…" I cry as I sputter saliva onto the cold floor. "Please, stop. Why are you doing this to me?" I ask as though I'd get a rational answer. People like Gabe don't think rationally. They have no moral compass.

The only compass Gabe has is hanging between his legs, and it's pointing straight at me.

"Blah, blah, blah. All you whores do is talk." He whines.

I can feel flecks of his spit against my legs as he talks. His hands smear grease and dirt across my legs as he crawls over me, closer and closer. The dread I felt when he first attacked me overtakes me again.

"Now be a good little whore and take what's coming to you." My body falls limp, and I close my eyes. Please stop. Please stop. "You're mine." He rasps.

"The fuck she is!"

The next sound I hear is a sickening crack of bone as a fist connects with Gabe's nose. It's Luke. Gabe doesn't even have a chance to react. Luke peels him off of me and tosses him to the floor. Gave skids across the floor and Luke pounces on him, unleashing a flurry of lefts and rights. A part of me wants Luke to keep going. I want Gabe to understand that he can't do this. He can't treat people this way and get away with it.

But another part of me is afraid that Luke won't stop until Gabe's dead.

I've never seen Luke act like this.

He's not who you think he is. Miles's words resound in my mind.

No! I throw myself on Luke. I won't let Luke do something stupid.

"Luke, stop!" I cry as I try to wrap my arms around him. He's too strong, and I barely offer any resistance to him. "Stop!

You'll kill him!" And I meant it too. Gabe has his arms up, trying to block Luke's punches. I can see blood on the Luke's fists.

Miles was already suspicious of Luke. What more reason did he need than this? Maybe he was right. I don't know what Luke is capable of.

But he stops seconds later.

"You're not worth it." He spits at Gabe as he grabs him by his shirt and pulls him to his feet; I stumble backward as he stands up. "If I so much as see you look at Leah again…" He drags Gabe to the front door and throws him out. There's a trail of blood drops that leads from me to the door.

Glass rattles and the floor shakes from the force at which Luke shuts the door. He stands there; his right hand still flat against it and his head down.

Chapter Fourteen
Leah

He saved me again.

Why am I always the one who needs saving? Why can't I be the hero for once? This is my life, and I'm tired of being the victim.

"Leah…" He begins, his back still facing me.

It has only been a week, but it feels like ages since I've heard his voice. It shouldn't be affecting me this way, but it is. It always has. It's warm and smooth and, above all, comforting. It's what I need right now.

He leans against the door and slides down to the floor. His hands hang limply over his knees.

"I should've taken you with me that night." He cups his face with his hands, then runs them through his hair and lets out a long, airy sigh.

"You had no other choice." I tell him.

"But I did." He snaps back. "I mean.

Sorry." His eyes flit over to mine. They're wet, but there aren't any tears. "I could've put up more of a fight. Then maybe—" He glances over at me again, longer this time. I know what he's looking at. My scar. I cover it with my hand, instinctively. "Maybe things would've turned out different." He looks back at his hands.

Maybe he's right. Maybe things could've worked out, but we can't change what happened. We can't sit here thinking about what could've been—it will tear us apart. I've come to terms with what happened. With my mother, with my father, with Luke, with everything.

And I'm tired of reliving the pain. I want to move on with my life. Forget this town and everything that happened to me and be happy. I want to live.

I walk over to him. His knees are up, and his head rests in between his hands as wild tufts of hair sprout in between his fingers. I kneel down beside him and place a hand on his shoulder. "There's nothing you could've done." I whisper, stroking his arm. My hand traces the outline of his musculature underneath his shirt and my mind flashes back to the night I saw him naked.

"I mean it." I reach out to touch his hand, but I stop myself. It's battered and bleeding from punching Gabe, and it's already beginning to swell. "Luke! We need to clean that!"

He shrugs. "It's not that bad." He holds his hand out in front of him and inspects it, almost in admiration. Small, meandering rivulets of red stain the back of his hand. There's dirt, probably from Gabe, smeared along one of his knuckles.

I can see the one corner of his mouth forming a smile.

Mr. Tough Guy.

But, to be honest, it was kind of hot how he saved me like that. I'll never tell him though; I wouldn't want to inflate his ego more than it already is.

"Not that bad? Luke James Hammond..."

I feel like a mother scolding a child as grab him by the arm and lead him into the kitchen.

"Sit." I instruct him, pointing to an open chair. He sits down and rests his bloody hand on the table. He leans back and stretches his other arm against the back of the chair. His V-neck shirt dips low enough to reveal part of his well-defined pecs. My eyes trace their outline and down to his abs. For a moment, I forget what I'm doing, lost in admiration, my heart fluttering.

I catch myself, but it's too late. The cocky grin of his returns as his cool blue eyes scan my body.

I leave for a moment to collect everything I need. "Am I going to make it, Doc?" He asks.

I let out a deep sigh, and ignore him.

The chair squeaks against the linoleum as I drag it toward him and sit down.

"Hand." I say, looking him in the eye.

"This feels familiar." He says, extending his hand to me. "Only I think our roles were reversed—*Aggh*!" He wrenches his hand away, but not before I doused his wound with alcohol. That's one way to shut him up. I smile contentedly at myself.

"Oh, stop being such a baby." I chide.

He snorts a laugh, offering his hand again. Holding it with my left hand, I wipe away the blood and clean his cuts with the other. His hand is firm, rough, and masculine, and I'm trying not to think about it all over my body.

Oops. Too late.

I can imagine the warmth of it, wrapping around the nape of my neck, cupping my breasts, spanking my ass. I can feel myself beginning to flush.

Don't look up. Don't look...

My eyes flit up to his, and he's not even attempting to hide the fact that he's looking down my shirt as I'm leaning over, caring for his wound. And I'm not attempting to hide that I like it.

I like that he finds me attractive.

I like that he calls me sexy.

I like how he protects me and will do anything for me.

But would he kill someone for you. His own mother?

No! I tell myself, dismissing the thought as soon as it rises to the surface. Luke isn't a killer. I couldn't possibly fall for a killer... could I?

"You know Miles thinks you killed Judith."

He laughs. "Of course he would. He's a terrible detective." I can feel his eyes on me. "Wait. How did you know that?"

"I saw him earlier today. He promised me that he'd return Judith's locket. That's the only reason I met with him." I let out a sigh, dropping my hands from his as I look at him. "But he said they didn't find a locket on her."

He grunts. "Weird."

"I know. I've searched this entire house, but it's not here." I return to bandaging his hand.

"Why do you want it, anyways?"

"To destroy it." I say, simply.

He laughs at me again. "Seriously?"

"I wanted to destroy the one thing she loved more than anything else."

He doesn't say anything. I'm almost done bandaging. I'm just finishing the wrapping when I add: "He has it out for you. He thinks you hurt Judith."

"Do you believe him?" He asks.

"No." I mean it, too.

Luke's free hand palms one side on my face. It's warm and comforting, and I can feel myself melting under his touch. I've ached for his touch for so long.

"Leah." His voice is low and rough, and I can feel it in my chest. My heart hammers as I look up at him, and he looks back at me. "Thanks." He smiles. A real smile, not his cocky, arrogant smile, but a real one. From the heart.

"I should be the one thanking you." I say with a snort. "I don't know what would've happened if you weren't here."

I can feel his hand tense up as I talk, and when I look up at him, I can see the rage welling up in his eyes, flushing through his skin. It was the same look I saw when he went for Gabe.

He cares for me. I know it. And after a week without seeing him, I know I care for him, too. But I guess I've always known that. I've always tried to ignore my feelings for Luke, always ran away from them when the welled up. That's a lot of running for one person when your bedrooms share a wall, when you see them day after day.

I can't do it anymore. I'm tired of it. I'm tired of running away from what I want.

I finish wrapping his hand and look back up at him. My breath catches in my chest. How could someone be so beautiful? My eyes flit across his handsome face, to his eyes, to his strong, stubbled jaw, to his wide chin, and then up to his lips.

I want to taste them again, feel them, wet against on my flesh. My tongue slides between my lips, anticipating, waiting.

"You're beautiful, Leah."

I can feel myself blush, and I look away.

"No need to be bashful, Leah."

I love the way he says my name. The way it rolls off his tongue, through his kissable lips and into my ears.

He takes my chin in between his thumb and forefinger and directs my gaze back to him. He brushes my lower lip gently with his thumb then cups my cheek with his hand. I can smell the trace amount of cologne on his wrist, along his pulse point and an overwhelming sense of happiness courses through me. Every happy memory of Luke rushes back through me. It's almost more joy than I can bear and I want to squeal. Jump up and down and dance like an idiot.

A lovestruck idiot.

"I mean it." He says without breaking eye contact or even blinking.

Gray. His eyes look slate gray at this distance with strands of blue. They're soft and compassionate eyes. Although, maybe passionate would be a better descriptor. Both of his eyes and of him. There's passion in everything he does. It shows in his eyes, in the way he carries himself. He's always had it. I admired him for it, envied him even because I never had that same passion. Or, I guess I should say: I had passion before. But it was stricken from me by Judith.

I always wanted to be an artist. I used to draw and paint all the time. I had passion. But it's hard to be passionate about anything when you have a stepmother like Judith. When she makes you second-guess your worth. Makes you feel insecure and worthless. It's draining. Demoralizing, even.

But now I can finally feel that part of me speak up. It's faint, but I can hear it when I see Luke. When I think about what the future may hold now that Judith's gone. Now that I'm free, finally escaping this vicious cycle I've been caught in for so long.

Right now, all I see is Luke.

His thumb circles my cheek gently as he holds my face in his hand; the rest of his fingers weave their way into my hair.

"I'm going to kiss you now." He tells me.

A smile flickers on my face as breath comes to me in quick bursts. There's no way he can't hear my heart beating; it's all I can hear right now. My head throbs with every beat, but I wouldn't have it any other way because… I'm happy.

I'm truly happy. It's strange thinking that, but even stranger feeling it. It has been a long time since I've felt this way.

I could get used to this.

"Okay," is all I can manage, but it's more than enough.

He leans in, and our lips touch. It's gentle at first, but then it evolves into something that is less a kiss than a forceful merging of two mouths. I can't tell where my mouth ends and his begins and at this point it doesn't even matter. Nothing matters except for this moment.

My hands find their way to his back, and I dig with my nails. They slide against his skin, and I can only imagine the red marks that now line his back. He doesn't flinch. Doesn't even care.

He grabs a fistful of my hair and pulls down. Our lips and tongues disentangle themselves from each other's, and I gasp for much-needed air.

My core is on fire, and my thoughts, incoherent. It's hard to think when someone as hot as Luke is making out with you.

His eyes dart across my face as he holds my hair like a mother cat holds her child by the scruff. I'm immobile—completely under his control—and I wouldn't have it any other way.

"You're so fucking sexy, Leah." He rasps.

His lips dive back in and my back arches reactively to his lips gently sucking my neck. My breath catches in my chest as he nibbles my earlobe.

"Luke, fuck me." I breathe as he kisses me along my collarbone. "Please." I beg.

He pulls away from me.

Did I say something wrong?

He stands up and swipes everything off the kitchen table behind us. Metal and glass crash to the floor. Then, in one fluid motion, he picks me up and sets me down on the space he just cleared.

"Ever been fucked on a table before?" He growls; his hands rip the front of my tank top in half as if it were paper.

I shake my head as I bite my lower lip. I'm so turned on by how strong he is, how animalistic and primal it all seems. I've never…

I've never felt this way before. My body is on fire.

"This won't be the last."

He pulls his shirt off over his head as I remove my tattered tank top. I can't tear my eyes away from his perfect v-taper or his abs. Nor what's underneath his pants, bulging, throbbing, inches in front of me.

His body is perfection.

I'm ruined. How can I go back to anyone else after this? Luke is a breed all his own—unmatched. Everyone after this will be mediocre at best. But I don't want to go back to anyone else. Luke is the only one I want.

"God damn, Leah. You're so sexy." He says as he pulls down my bra. "I can't control myself when I'm around you."

I fling my head back as his lips encircle my pebbled nipple, sucking hard. He nibbles them gently, sending short, quick bursts of pleasure through me.

But those quick bursts are overshadowed as I feel Luke's hand find its way to my mound.

"Oh, fuck!" I squeal as his middle finger slides over my nub, shockwaves spreading throughout my body.

"You like that?"

I can't talk. I can't think. All I can do is feel, feel my orgasm welling up inside me.

He slides a finger inside me.

"Come for me, Leah."

My body begins to quiver and shake as I come on his fingers.

"That's it." He says, his finger still working its magic inside me. He pulls away from my quivering body.

"Now strip." He demands.

Still reeling, I remove my bra and toss it to the floor. I watch as it falls, landing where they found Judith. My stomach feels sick. I don't want the first time Luke fucks me to be tainted by her.

"Wait." I say.

"What?"

I nod to where they found Judith. He looks over his shoulder and shakes his head.

"Your room or mine?"

I don't even have to think about it. I've fantasized about this for so long that it comes out instantaneously. "Yours."

I want to see what it's like to be on the other side of the wall, to be the one who's screaming his name, not listening to it.

He grabs my hand and pulls me into him. We stumble backward as we kiss. I can feel his hard cock through his pants, rubbing against my stomach. I grab onto it as we continue our slow dance to his bedroom.

We hardly make it out of the kitchen before he says, fuck it, and throws me onto the couch.

I fall onto my back, and he kneels down in front of me. He fingers the band of my panties and pulls them off, tossing them behind his head.

My back arches and my legs grip Luke's head in between them as his pursed lips find my sensitive nub. My body shakes and writhes, attempting to deal with the sensory overload.

"I'm… I'm.."

Noises I've never made before come from my mouth as my body shakes. No one has ever made me come this hard. I look down and see Luke's eyeing me, that cocky smirk back on his face. He knows what he's doing. He's done it to so many girls before me. And right now, I don't even care.

"Enjoying yourself?"

Enjoying myself? Hah! He knows damn well I'm enjoying myself as I'm laying here, still writhing, still basking in the pleasurable afterglow.

"No?" He asks, playfully, in response to my silence. "I guess I should get going then."

"Luke!" I squeal as he begins to stand up. There's that grin again. And there it goes, igniting my center.

"Just kidding."

He pounces on me and we kiss. It's rough and forceful and everything I never thought I'd want from a kiss. Our tongues dance and twist, exploring each other's mouth while Luke's hand is wrapped around my throat, pinning me to the couch.

I wrap my legs around him as my nails dig new lines into his back.

My lips break away from his and I whisper, "Fuck me."

His eyes flit to mine and then moments later, I feel his cock thrust deep inside me.

"You're so tight, Leah." He growls as his hands grip tight against my waist, pulling me, guiding me closer to him.

"You feel so good inside me." The couch scrapes against the floor with each thrust; the lamp on the end table next to us crashes to the floor.

It's happening again. That feeling. That incredible orgasm. It's building. Deeper this time and even more intense.

I look up at Luke, he's straining, nearing

the same edge as me but he doesn't stop. In and out, in and out, deeper and deeper until I can't bear it anymore.

It washes over me, everything around me seems to fade. I feel Luke's cock pulsate inside me as he fills me with his seed, leaving my body quivering, aching for more.

He collapses on me and we lay on the couch together, entangled in each other's arms.

We stay like that for a while until he finally breaks the silence.

"Leah." He whispers into my ear. His breath is warm against my skin.

"Yes?"

"I want you to live with me." My heart flutters and my breath hitches because I want the same thing. I want to get out of this town, go somewhere far, far away and begin again. A new life and a fresh start.

Luke, although he can be domineering at times, he can also be sweet. And he truly does want the best for me. I've been so caught up with something that happened years ago, that I misunderstood, that I've been blinded to the good in him. All I saw was the bad, exaggerated it even. I painted a picture of him that wasn't entirely true.

Besides, what do I really have to lose by going with him? It will get me out of this town, away from the past I can't seem to outrun. If things go sour, I could leave.

But are you certain he didn't kill his own mother? The more rational part of me questions.

There's no way Luke would ever harm anyone. Well, except for Gabe. That was different. He attacked me. Twice.

How different is Gabe from Judith? She's been poisoning you for years. It retorts.

No. I'm not afraid of Luke.

Everything Miles told me was circumstantial.

"I can get you a job, get you back on your feet." He strokes my head. Goose bumps pop up on my arms and back. "No strings attached. If it doesn't work out, or if you want something different, I'll help you with whatever you need. I promise. I just want to make it up to you for not being there. What do you think?"

I think I'm going to say yes. Scratch that. Of course, I'm going to say yes. But I don't want him to see how excited I am.

I flip over to face him. His eyes soften as he looks at me.

"Can I think about it?" I ask, even though I know I won't have to.

"Take all the time you need." He tells me as he twirls a tendril of hair around one of his fingers.

I lay my head flat against his chest and think for the first time in my life everything will be okay. Everything is going to be fine.

I close my eyes and fall asleep.

CHAPTER FIFTEEN
LEAH

I COULDN'T HAVE BEEN asleep for more than a few minutes before I hear a loud pounding on the

"This is the police!" A voice booms from the other side of the door. "Open up." It demands. "We have a warrant for the arrest of Luke Hammond."

The expressions on both of our faces are: What the fuck is going on?

My heart hammers in unison with the pounding on the door. This can't be happening. Why is this happening?

"It's going to be okay," Luke says, trying to comfort me. "I promise." He takes my face in his hands as tears stream down my cheeks. The pounding on the door, the booming of voices outside, all of it is drowned out by Luke's voice. He's all I see, all I hear. "I need you to take my phone. Call Gretchen and have her contact my lawyer. Everything will be sorted in a few hours."

He grabs his pants from the floor and

retrieves his phone from his pocket. He hands it to me. My hands are shaky and I nearly drop it. "Call Gretchen." He repeats with stern eyes and an even sterner voice. "Now go. Head upstairs before they see you."

His eyes scan my body one last time before he puts on his pants.

I can't run upstairs and hide; they'd see me through the window. I walk to the dining room behind us. It's of sight from the front door, but close enough for me to hear whatever happens. I lean back against the wall, clutching Luke's phone against my chest, then slide down to the floor.

"Well, howdy officers." Luke lilts as he opens the door. "What can I do you for?"

Why wasn't he taking this seriously? I mean, this wasn't something to take lightly. Miles is hellbent on pinning this murder on him, no matter how circumstantial the evidence is.

"Luke Hammond," a voice I don't recognize booms. "You're under arrest for the assault of Gabe Harris and for the suspected murder of Judith Hammond."

"Is this funny to you, Luke?" Another voice asks. Miles's voice.

I can hear Luke chuckling as handcuffs zip around his wrists. "That you think I'd waste energy on Gabe without reason? That you think I killed Judith. Yeah. It is funny, detective."

I want to rush out there, tell Miles that he's wrong, that Luke saved me from Gabe and that he never laid a finger on Judith. But it wouldn't help. Not to mention, I'd have to find a way to explain why I'm completely naked while my stepbrother is half-naked.

Instead, I sit here. Sit against the cold wall and wait for them to leave so I can call Gretchen and figure out what the hell to do about everything.

I thought everything was going to be fine. Why couldn't I just run away with Luke. Why is the rug always ripped out from under me when something good finally happens to me. I tap the back of my head against the wall as I wait for them to leave.

I don't have to wait long. They're gone within minutes.

I look down at Luke's phone and touch the screen. It prompts me to enter the passcode.

"Seriously?" I say to the empty room.

I fling my head back and sigh. Why

didn't he tell me the passcode? Seriously.

I rack my brains, trying to figure out what it could be.

I enter his name: 5853. Denied.

I enter his birthday: 3991. Denied.

Maybe… : 5324. Denied. My name. Wishful thinking, I guess.

I drop the phone on the floor and kick it away from me. It slides and spins across the floor. I don't know what to do. I guess I should probably get some clothes on and head down to the station. They'd let me see him, right? At the very least I could ask them to get the code to his phone from him. Something. He gets one phone call though, right?

I let out a deep sigh.

I look at the phone as it sits against the wall on the other side of the room.

One last shot. I'll give it one last shot before I go.

With the phone in my hand, I enter the final combination that comes to mind: 7791. My birthday.

The numbers disappear and I'm met with a picture of both of us on the home screen.

We're at the beach, our skin, sun-kissed, and wind blowing in our hair wildly. I remember that day. It was one of the few times I was happy. Actually happy. All of us spent the day at Galveston beach. It's not the best beach by any means, but it was the closest and we made the best of it. We were so burned by the end of it that it even bending an arm or leg was painful. But you can't tell that from the photograph.

I was happy. Happy that I was spending time with Luke.

I shake myself out of it as I remember what I need to do: Call Gretchen.

I get her on the phone and tell her everything that happened. Well, most of it anyway. I skipped the part where Luke fucked me, even though a part of me wanted to hear her reaction.

She probably wouldn't have believed it anyway. Whatever. She's on her way over now, and she's getting in touch with Luke's lawyer.

All I have to do is wait for her. Just wait.
Tick. Tock. Tick. Tock.

How the hell can I do that when Luke's locked up? I can't just sit here and wait. I want to do something. Ugh. But there's nothing I can do. With my luck, I'll somehow find a way to make things worse.

Gretchen's right. I just need to sit here and wait.

After retrieving my clothes and dressing, changing my ripped tank top for another, I head back downstairs.

There's a knock on the door before I reach the bottom step.

It's Mrs. O'Malley. Her hair looks silver in the moonlight.

I smile at her as I open the door. I ask how she's doing and a smile flickers on her face.

"Oh, call me Constance, dear. None of this Mrs. O'Malley." She waves her arm in front of her as though she's batting a fly. "I'm fine, anyways. How are you?" Her voice is soft but strangely comforting.

When my Judith forced me to stop eating sugary foods, I'd often stop by Mrs. O'Malley's house. She always had a pan of brownies or a sheet of cookies ready to offer me. Something sweet and tasty.

Her sweet child. That's what she'd always call me. I didn't mind. I liked her company and the sweets. She felt like more of a mother to me than Judith ever did. She even visited me at Millwood more than Judith.

"Well," I sigh, shrugging my shoulders and then letting them fall limply. "Not good." I tilt my head as I look at her.

"Oh, of course, sweet child. I can't imagine how difficult it has been for you these past few days. Your mother was a sweet woman." I want to stop her right there, but I hold back. She wouldn't understand. "And judging from the ruckus earlier," she continues, waving her hand in the air as she looks around her, "bad luck just seems to follow you. Come here."

She sticks her hands out and beckons me with her bony fingers. She wraps her arms around me and I do the same.

"Now, I'm just about to take out a fresh batch of brownies." She whispers to me. "How about you come over and have one." We break from our hug.

"Oh, I'm not sure." I should probably stay here and wait for Gretchen, but what's the harm in a brownie? Besides, she won't be here for another hour or so. I'll be back by then.

"I won't take no for and answer." She jokes with her hands on her hips and her eyebrows raised.

"Oh, alright," I relent, feigning

exasperation. "I can't say no to a brownie, especially yours. Are there chocolate chips?"

"Are there chocolate chips, she says?" She repeats through a laugh. She grabs my arm and leads me down the steps.

"Of course! And you won't say no to seconds either!" She pipes back, jabbing a finger at me.

Chapter Sixteen
Leah

I'VE BEEN HERE LESS than 10 minutes and I've already eaten three brownies. Three! They're just so warm and gooey and fresh. Constance was right, I couldn't say no to seconds… or thirds…

Fourths? I'm not addicted. I promise.

I don't know how she does it. I'll have to get the recipe.

"Another one, dear?" She calls to me from the kitchen. My hands clench the sofa as I rock back and forth, reeling from my sugar high. As much as I want to say yes, I tell her no.

"Well, at the very least, let me refill your milk." She swoops in and whisks away my glass before disappearing back into the kitchen.

My eyes wander around the room. It's what you'd expect from someone her age—whatever that may be.

Old, frayed wingback chairs flank a large wood-burning fireplace; quilts with floral patterns, color fading from them, hang from the chairs. There's a strange assortment of knickknacks and pictures collecting dust on the mantle above the fireplace. A battered china hutch filled with unused plates and saucers and cups looms to my right, next to the kitchen. Springs creak and whine as I shift my body on the avocado green couch.

Everything is dated and covered with a thin layer of dust and old-person smells.

I'm waiting for a cat or ten to spring out at me somewhere.

But, that doesn't happen, so I'm a little disappointed.

I stand up and walk to the mantle. There's a portrait of a girl at the far end that attracts my eye. She seems strangely familiar and I can't place why.

"My daughter, Abigail." Constance says wistfully as she places the milk on the coffee table. I nearly jump at the sound of her voice. "She was a darling. My sweet child."

She walks to my side and places one hand on my back. "She's always reminded me of you." She touches Abigail's face with her finger, leaving a clean, dustless circle on the glass. "I remember when you first moved in. I thought I was losing my mind. I thought my Abigail was back."

I can see some resemblance. We have the same hair and eyes, even our smiles. It's strange how I never noticed it before. But I guess I never paid much attention to the decor. Not when brownies are on the table…

"But it was a fool's dream." She lets out a heavy sigh and takes the frame from my hand. "She passed long ago."

"I'm so sorry."

"Oh, it wasn't a surprise. She wasn't a healthy child. Always sick." Her voice sounds distant and weak. She places the picture back on the mantle, stares at it for a moment then turns back to me. A faint smile flickers on her mouth. "You'd think as a nurse, I'd be able to care for my own child."

I never knew she was a nurse. Although I guess now that I think about it, I don't really know all that much about her.

"We both know what it's like to lose someone we love."

"Yes." I was thinking about my father. Not Judith.

I was beginning to feel light-headed, so I sit back down on the couch. Constance sits beside me. She smells of flour and chocolate and something else I can't place.

Her hand finds my knee and she asks me, "How are you coping, dear?"

"It's been tough," I tell her. "But Luke has been helping me through it."

She seems to tense up when I say his name.

"Oh, that's nice, dear." She tells me through gritted teeth. I can sense she doesn't mean it, but I don't know why. She seemed spooked by him the night my Judith died. Like she knows something I don't. "I saw the police taking him away in handcuffs." She says airily as she hands me my glass. I grab it and take a gulp without even thinking if I'm thirsty or not. It's what you do, I guess. When someone like Constance offers you something, you take it. Even if you don't want it. Even if…

The dizziness is getting worse. My hand shakes and I spill some of the milk on my shirt.

"Oh, sweet child. I'm so sorry. You're going through enough as it is. And here I am dredging it back up." She slaps her hands against her thighs. "I'm so sorry."

"No." I shake my head, trying to get my bearings. "It's okay. I'm just feeling a little queasy."

"Oh, no." She wraps an arm around me while the back of her other hand grazes against my cheek. "Why don't you go to my bathroom and get yourself a little something to settle your stomach. I'll be right in to help you if you need it."

I tell her okay and get to my feet. I'm a little shaky, but okay. I can walk just fine, but my head I beginning to pound.

It must be the stress. So much has happened that my body was bound to shut down at some point. It always does.

I brace myself against Constance's medicine cabinet for a moment and close my eyes. Even the light is beginning to be too much.

Constance has enough bottles and vials and tubes that she'd have no problem running a small pharmacy out of her house.

I never want to get old.

I rummage through the bottles, reading one label after another. The names seem to be written in another language—so foreign and complex. I can't find Advil, or Tylenol, or even aspirin. Nothing is recognizable except for…

Except for…

Fear grabs hold of me and I drop the

bottles I'm holding. The pills rattle in them as they bounce around in the sink.

My eyes flit to a small vial, reading it as Constance calls to me. "Is everything alright in there, dear?"

"Ye—Yes." I sputter as I back out of the bathroom, my hands clinging tightly against my chest.

The same drugs that were found in Judith's toxicology report are in Constance's medicine cabinet.

This can't be happening. This can't be true. Judith was…

The room is spinning and I trip and fall onto the bed.

I can't move. My muscles feel heavy. Everything is…

Constance walks into the room. She's wearing Judith's nightgown and her locket.

Get up. Get out of here. Now!

But it's too late. My vision's becoming blurry; there's a haziness covering everything around me.

The last thing I hear before everything fades to black is Constance.

"I hate seeing my sweet child sick." She coos.

And the last thing I feel is her cold, bony

hand as it brushes against my cheek.

PART FOUR

Chapter Seventeen
Luke

The drunk tank.

They put me in the fucking drunk tank. There are no benches, no place to sit. The air is acrid with the scent of urine and I'm sure the floor is covered in it as well as any number of other bodily fluids. The floor is a sticky mess and each time I lift a foot, it feels as though I'm peeling velcro from the bottom of my shoe.

Miles thinks I killed Judith. Says he has proof, too. It's as much amusing as it is alarming. What proof? I didn't kill her. Scout's honor. Hell, ever since I found out she was dead, I assumed she swallowed a bottle of sleeping pills, chased it with a bottle of wine. She wasn't the most stable person. It seemed like something Judith would do. The final passive-aggressive act: *Do you see what you did to me? You did this to me. I had no other choice. It's not me; it's you.*

Adamant until the very end.

Proof… It's all a bluff. Throwing me in here with some bullshit charge, trying to wear me down. It's a game. He has nothing but a hunch and he's hoping I'll give something up. But the truth is that I have nothing to offer. No information that will blow this case open. I didn't kill Judith and I have no idea who did.

I'm leaning against the back wall, my arms folded across my waist, waiting. Waiting for the whistling, corpulent officer with sausage link fingers and mustard stained lips to slink down the narrow corridor, open the door, and tell me I'm free to go.

It should be any minute now. Leah should've already called Gretchen, and Gretchen should've contacted my lawyer. Any minute now. Or so I think.

How long have I been in here? Fifteen minutes? An hour? Five? It's hard to say. Time seems to stand still in a place like this; it's a separate world governed by its own set of rules. I've never been behind bars before now, and I don't plan on being behind them for much longer. Or ever again, for that matter.

The only thing keeping me sane is thinking about Leah and the moment we shared. I'm counting the minutes until I can hold her in my arms, taste her lips. I can imagine the softness of her lips pressed against mine.

I never intended to fall for her, but that's how it works, right? No matter how much you plan, life has its own way of doing things. I've decided it's best not to question it. At least, not all the time.

When this all blows over in the next hour or so—hopefully, sooner—I'll take Leah and we'll leave Milton for good. She may choose to go her own separate way sometime after that, but that's her choice. I only want the best for her and if that means she wants something or someone else, so be it.

She's been through hell and I'm not about to put her through it again.

But I hope she chooses to stay. We could be great together, and there's no one else I can imagine by my side than her.

I let out a heavy sigh and raise my head to look around the rectangular cell once again.

There are two other men. Both of them were here before me. One's mumbling incoherently to himself in the back corner to my right, high on something.

He's a ragged man. Stringy, long brown hair falls in dirty clumps on his shoulders. He waves his dirt-smeared hands animatedly in front of him as though in a heated argument with an invisible person. Every now and then he lets out a wicked laugh. The type of laugh that's more unnerving than it is comforting. A mad man's cackle.

To be honest, I'm surprised that there aren't more like him in here.

You would think that larger cities—Austin, New York, Boston, wherever—would have worse drug problems than Milton. That may be the case. More people, more drugs. But the problem is more or less hidden. Swept under the rug, so to speak. You could go days, weeks, months, hell, even years, without seeing someone doped up.

In Milton? There's not much space to hide. It's out in the open.

In the bigger cities, the drug addicts are nameless. Degenerates with whom you share no connection. Here, they're your neighbors, the people who serve you in diners, the guy who bags your groceries at the local market.

The boy next door. The preacher's daughter.

You know them, or are at least familiar with them.

Sometimes I'm glad that Robert kicked me out when he did. It was a blessing of sorts. This town seems to have a toxic effect on people. You might be able to fight it off for a time, but sooner or later it will infect you in some form or another.

No one's immune. Not even me.

The old man squeals as he thrusts a spindly arm in front of him.

"Oh shut up you haggard fuck!" The other man (hell, he couldn't be more than a day over 21) shouts with a drunken slur across the cell. He's rail thin. His thinness is accentuated by the baggy clothing that hangs from him like sheets on a clothesline. A stick figure. Two beady black eyes under thick black eyebrows glare across the room at the old man who seems unaware of anything but the conversation he's having with himself.

"Jesus fucking Christ…" He breathes, bringing his hands to his head, massaging his temples.

I snort and shake my head.

"The fuck you laughing at?" He spits at me.

His eyebrows form a thick line across his forehead as he stares at me, his mouth open in a snarl.

I shrug and shift myself so my back is turned to him. The last thing I needed was another altercation. It would only complicate my already complicated situation. What's a silly kid to me?

"That's what I thought."

I smile creeps onto my face. I like this kid's spunk. A little overconfident, but that's better than being timid. Unfortunately for him, he needs the bite to back up his bark. Judging by his frame, he doesn't have it. He'll have a tough lesson to learn if he keeps up with that mouth in the form of a swift punch to the jaw. I won't be the one to teach him though. I need to get out of here.

I let out a sigh and focus on Leah.

Not much later, I hear the steady thump of rubber soles against the concrete floor. The thumps turn into thuds as the guard gets closer. He's not whistling but as he comes into view, he licks his mustard stained lips as his sausage link fingers fumble to open up the door to the cell.

"Luke Hammond," He snarls, his eyes darting around the cell until he spots me. "You're free to go."

I follow my corpulent friend in blue as he guides me down the narrow corridor and through a few doors until finally leaving me at a window to collect my things.

"Name?" The lady asks. She's older. Her auburn hair, pulled back behind her head, is striped with thin streaks of gray. She wears thick, horn-rimmed glasses and looked more like a librarian than a police officer.

"Hammond. Luke Hammond." I smile.

She rolls her eyes and retrieves the few items I had when I came in.

"Sign here." She says, shoving a clipboard with a form that has far too many words on it. Signature on the line. No problem.

Moments later I'm out the door, stretching my stiff muscles and breathing in fresh, clean air. There's a faint sound of sirens in the distance, but otherwise it's calm, relaxing even. In a few short hours Leah and I will be out of here.

But where is she?

Something about this didn't make sense.

Actually, a lot of this didn't make sense. I would've expected to see Miles, fuming at my release. Not to mention Dave, my lawyer who'd be wearing a satisfied, shit-eating grin.

But no one is here. Something is wrong.

I check with the officer at the front desk to see if I can talk with Miles. He's not here, the man tells me. I could leave a message if I'd like and he'd make sure he'd give it to him when he returns.

Great.

Where the hell was Leah? And Gretchen? And Dave? They were the ones who got me out of here, right? Who else could have? Nothing was adding up, but I found myself walking aimlessly toward the house.

I'm no more than a 100 feet from the police station when Gretchen's BMW screeches around a corner and parks in front of the station. She stumbles out of the car, her hair wild, some of it matted against her cheeks, and slams the door behind her. She trips over the curb and onto the grass.

"Gretchen!" I yell, waving my arms.

Her eyes dart around as she tries to locate me. I jog over to her; she's still sitting on the damp grass when I get there. The smudged makeup around her eyes make her look like a raccoon and her eyes are bloodshot and puffy. I've never seen her like this before. She won't even look at me.

"Gretchen," I say as calmly as possible. "What's going on?"

She sniffles. Her shoulders heave along with her chest as she takes ragged, breaths. I'm afraid she might hyperventilate.

"Just calm down." I kneel down and rub her shoulder. "Take deep breaths and relax."

It seems to work. Once she starts focusing on her breathing the tears stop streaming down her cheeks and she finally looks at me.

"Leah." She rasps.

"What about Leah?"

"She's... She's..." She looks away from me. I look down and see that she's pulling fistfuls of grass from the ground. I place my hand on hers, stopping her from pulling anymore.

I lower my gaze and force Gretchen to look at me. "Gretchen. I need you to tell me what's going on."

Her eyes get wider and it seems as though she's looking through me, not at me.

"We have to go. Now."

Chapter Eighteen
Leah

It's dark.

I can't see anything except for the sliver of light that shines underneath the door and the yellow cone it paints on the carpet. The room smells damp and musty, mildewed cloth and the various odors that have been collecting in the old carpet over the years. My limbs feel heavy; I try to lift them, but they aren't responding to my commands. I can't sit up. My head... my stomach, too, they both ache horribly and I feel strange. Not myself. It feels as though I'm floating—no—like I'm on a rollercoaster; there's so much movement and I swear I'm going to fall through the bed at any moment.

Where am I?

I'm trying to gather my bearings, trying to remember where I am—how I got here.

Oh my god! I can't even remember how I got here.

I grimace as I turn my head—it's so painful, but I need to find something familiar, some sort of marker that will tell me where I am. The mildew smell, I determine, is coming from my nightgown.

When did I get dressed in this? I don't even own a nightgown.

The door begins to creak and slowly open. I watch as light begins to fill the room. I can see a bureau, the wrought iron bed I'm lying on, and a bathroom in which the medicine cabinet is open.

I'm struck by a sense of *deja vu*. There's something tugging on a memory in the corner of my mind, pulling it to the surface.

When I see the silhouette of a crooked figure coming through the doorway, it hits me. Constance. She fed me something that made me sick and black out. Abigail. The picture of her daughter. And the drugs in the medicine cabinet—the same drugs that were in my stepmother's body when she died. I remember…

Silverware and cups and bowls rattle and clank against each other as Constance, no longer a silhouette, carries a long, metal tray through the door. "I've got just the thing for you, Abigail."

Abigail. She called me Abigail. She thinks I'm her daughter, her dead daughter. But she couldn't possibly think that, could she? How crazy is she? This is only a dream. This is only a dream. This. Is. Only. A. Dream.

I repeat the words over and over in my head, but I know when I open my eyes I'll have to face the reality. This isn't a dream. This is my life. And it's slowly slipping away from me.

The throbbing pain in my head is becoming unbearable and now my stomach is beginning to cramp, along with nearly every muscle in my body. I grimace just as Constance sets down the tray beside me on the nightstand.

"Oh, my sweet child," she coos. Her eyes soften as she looks at me. "Mama's here." I can see Judith's locket hanging from her neck as she bends over and strokes my cheek. I twist my head, trying to squirm away from her touch.

"Now, now." She says. "Let's not be difficult."

She turns her attention to the tray.

I don't know what to do. Do I feed her

delusions? Play the part and hope that someone comes for me? Someone will come for me; I'm sure of it. Gretchen! She said she'd be here in a few hours. But, I don't know how much time has passed since I blacked out—an hour? Three? More? No. She'll come.

"Please. Just let me go. I promise I won't tell anyone. I won't tell anyone about this. Just please let me go." I beg. But as soon as the words leave my mouth, I realize how useless they are. Pleading with someone who poisons a girl she believes to be her daughter brought back from the dead? Yeah, that'll work.

The spoon in her hand clinks against the cup as she stirs its contents, whistling a soft, mellow tune—a lullaby.

Hush, little baby, don't say a word, mama's gonna buy you a mockingbird.

I can feel the heaviness of my limbs disappear, replaced by a tingling sensation that emanates from my fingers and toes and runs through my calves, through my forearms. I try to move again. I twist and turn, writhe and wriggle, but it's no use. As the tingling subsides, my ankles and wrists feel sore. I look to the right and see a thin, brown leather strap run from the under the covers and disappear underneath the bed. The strap moves as I move my hand. I'm strapped to the bed.

I'm in a waking nightmare. This can't be real. How could anyone do this to another person?

And if that mockingbird won't sing, mama's gonna...

"Now, Abigail, you mustn't fuss. You need to rest. You're not well and you need your strength. But don't worry, Mother will make everything better."

She returns to the drink she's creating on the nightstand, resumes humming her lullaby.

Forget begging, forget feeding her delusions; there's no telling what would happen if I went along with her little fantasy.

"Abigail is dead Constance. You said so yourself. You're not my mother." I could feel my skin warm up as the words flowed through me.

I could detect a slight change in her demeanor. She was agitated, but she was trying hard not to let it show; her right eyelid now twitches every few seconds and her hands shake as she spoons liquid into the cup. But, other than the nervous tic, there's no response. She continues mixing the drink.

Anger begins to rise in me; it's like nothing I've ever felt before. "I'm not your fucking daughter!" I scream, as I being to flail wildly on the bed, adrenaline pumping through me.

She drops the glass container and spoon she holds and they clank loudly against the metal tray, causing her concoction to topple over, some of it landing on my face. I taste a bit of it but sputter. It's disgusting, bitter.

She turns to me and looks at me with a faint, wistful smile. Her eyelids have sagged, nearly collapsing in on her eyes with age. I can sense sadness and pain in her eyes but also anger. So much anger. She fingers a stray tendril of gray hair away from her cheek, behind her ear. Then she takes the back of her hand and places it against my forehead.

"You're feverish, my dear. No wonder you're putting up such a fuss."

"You poisoned me and strapped me to a bed, forcing me to live in your fantasy world. You're wondering why I'm "putting up such a fuss? Feverish? No, I'm fucking terrified!"

"Language, Abigail!" Her eyes harden and she slaps me across my cheek. My vision flashes white as a jagged pain courses through my skull. The slap wasn't very hard, but it forced my head to jerk to the side, exacerbating my already splitting headache. I let out a low wail as tears well in my eyes.

"Now look what you made me do." Constance coos as she strokes my tender cheek with the back of her hand.

"You're sick," I whisper, eyes still shut tight. As the pain subsides, I slowly open them. Constance pulls on the locket with her thumb and forefinger, rubs it as she looks down at me with her sad, old eyes.

"It's worse than I imagined. You're really not well, Abigail." She pats my arm then brushes a stray hair from my face. "No, that medicine just isn't working. We're going to need something else to calm you down." She stands up, wringing her hands in front of her as she looks absently around the room for a moment. She lifts a finger in the air, pivots so she's facing a large wooden bureau, and says, "And I have just the thing."

Hush little baby, don't say a word...

Although she has a slight hunch, her

movements are swift and precise, graceful even. There's nothing I can do but watch her as she rifles through the drawers, tossing blankets and empty bottles behind her. But then she stops. She turns slowly around, staring at the two bottles in her hand. One is large, the size and shape of a vinegar bottle but white and opaque. The other is an orange, translucent bottle with a white cap. She lifts her eyes without moving her head and a wicked smile appears on her face before she begins whistling again.

And if that mockingbird won't sing...

She sets the bottles down on the tray before picking it up. She looks down at me and winks. "I'll be right back, dear."

Mama's gonna buy you a diamond ring...

I tug again at the restraints, but it's no use. I can scream and yell until I'm hoarse, but it won't do any good. No one's in my house, and no one has lived in the house next to Constance for years. No one will hear me.

The skin on my wrists is tender and raw, scarlet I'm sure. It's painful, but nothing I'm not used to and nothing compared to the splitting, dizzying headache; it keeps getting worse. I've grown accustomed to pain in various forms—physical, emotional—and in varying degrees. But there's still only so much a person can bear, and I think I've reached my limit, or I'm at the least looking over the edge.

I close my eyes and the warm tears that were beginning to pool in my eyes now stream down my cheeks, salty rivulets. I don't know if it's the drugs coursing through me right now or what but I'm exhausted. Every muscle aches and I just want to sleep. Maybe if I sleep I'll wake up in my own room; I'll wake up and this will all be over —never happened, actually—and everything will be okay.

The doorbell rings.

Gretchen! It has to be.

This is my chance. My one and only chance. I yell; I wail and scream as loud as possible in an attempt to let whoever is at the door, Gretchen or not, that someone is in trouble. Who cares about words, just make the loudest noise possible.

Constance is almost a blur as she swiftly crosses the room, one arm outstretched towards me. There's something in her hand, but I can't tell what it is—I don't have time.

I keep yelling and screaming for help, for someone to rescue me.

I feel a slight prick on my neck,

"No need to yell. Mama's here."

The already dim light grows dimmer as consciousness fades away.

Chapter Nineteen
Luke

"Gretchen, what the hell is going on?" The question glances off of her as she hops into the driver's seat. I open the passenger side door and follow suit. "Seriously." She's unresponsive. Her grip on the wheel is so tight that her knuckles have turned the same shade of white as her face. Silent tears stream down her face as she turns her head to me.

"It's Leah." Although she's sitting right next to me, I can hardly hear her. There's a jagged edge to her voice. Her grip on the steering wheel drops and the rest of her body seems to follow, crumbling in front of me as she breaks down again.

"Hey… Hey… It's okay." I say, pattering on her back and then rubbing it as she continues to sob. Gretchen was strong; in the two years that I've worked with her, I've seen her handle a workload that would drive a normal person toward a mental breakdown, but not her. Gretchen not only accepted everything that was handed to her, she didn't even break a sweat completing each and every task efficiently, even enthusiastically.

An ill feeling rushes over me, covers me —a blanket of discomfort.

"Leah called me." She begins, still sniffling. "Said you were in jail and that I needed to call your lawyer." She leans back and I slide my hand away. Her eyes are glassy, wet with tears, and she's staring absently in front of her. "So I did. She didn't give me any specifics, but it seemed like nothing serious. I decided to drive over anyway because I wanted to help." She rubs her left forearm with her hand, then starts fiddling with her fingers. "So that's what I did." She looks at me, then back at her hands. "I went to find Leah, but when I got to her house, no one was there. The lights were still on, and the door was unlocked, so I went inside. It was completely empty, but there was *blood*… someone's *blood*… all over the floor." Her eyes dart to my bandaged hand and up to my eyes before turning away.

"I called your phone, but it went straight to voicemail. I used your account to locate your phone. I thought she might have gone to the police station. But when I checked the app, it showed that the phone was next door." She turns her head and falls sideways against the door.

Next door? What does Constance have to do with this? The uneasiness within me spreads, increases in intensity until I can no longer ignore it.

"Gretchen, I need you to tell me what happened to Leah."

After a moment of silence, Gretchen looks at me finishes the rest of her story. When she went next door to see if Leah was there, she had no idea that her knocks were going to be answered by cries for help. She called 911 and no more than 5 minutes later the street again lit up with red and blue flashing lights. But it wasn't quick enough.

She was wheeled out on a stretcher by one medic while another pumped air into her lungs through a bag valve mask. They didn't tell her any more than what she saw except that Leah was being life flighted to St. David's Medical Center in Austin. While she was working on getting more information from one of the officers, she watched as a lady, silver-haired and unimposing, was lead out of the house and into a squad car.

Constance.

The only other bit of information the police gave her was about my release. They were dropping charges. I was free to go; no lawyer necessary.

Given the circumstances there's only one conclusion to draw, but I still don't understand it. Why would Constance harm Leah, kill Judith?

But, that's where we're at. Too many questions with even more unsatisfying answers.

I'M ONLY VAGUELY AWARE of the people around me as I move through the doors to St. David's and make my way into the waiting room. They all blur into one unintelligible mass of color. Even Gretchen, who follows at my heels, is fading away into the background, everything subordinate to my goal of reaching Leah.

The nurse behind the desk holds the telephone and speaks into the receiver in a low whisper. I don't have time to wait.

"Leah Hammond. Where is she?"

She looks up at me as though I'm crazy. She points toward a plastic sign sitting on the desk with her free hand then returns to her phone call. The red, bolded text on the sign states that visiting hours are over and then lists the hours.

I bend over and tilt my head so I'm looking directly at the nurse's eyes. "I don't give a *fuck* about visiting hours. You will tell me where Leah Hammond is or I will open every fucking door in this building until I find her. Your choice." I can feel Gretchen tugging at my arm.

"Sir, please step away from the desk. Visiting hours are over. If you don't need medical attention, I'm going to have to ask you to leave. Or I'll inform security and they can escort you off the premises." Her response is almost mechanical, as though I'm the tenth person who told her that today.

"Luke, come on. We need to go or else —"

"Or else what? I'll get arrested?" I snarl at Gretchen. Her face turns bright red and appears to shrink as she looks away. I was probably a little too curt, a little too harsh, but nothing else matter but getting to Leah.

I turn back to the nurse. She's off the phone now and writing something down on a clipboard.

"Who's her doctor. Let me speak with her doctor at least."

She looks at me as though I'm boring her. She sighs and asks for Leah's name again.

"I'll see if the doctor's available. Please take a seat." She motions to the empty seats along the wall.

I'VE BEEN WAITING FOR at least half an hour, at least, I think I have. My mind has been a mess of thoughts, both terrible and good, but all involving Leah. It's hard to believe that Leah's in the hospital. It wasn't long ago that she was in my arms, both of us thinking about the future and what I had in store for us. But now it's all up in the air.

Everything faded away again while I was lost in thought, so It took a few moments to notice that Gretchen was shaking me. Everything comes back into focus as Gretchen speaks, "Luke! Luke! Dr. Madison is here."

"Hello, Mr. Hammond. I'm Dr. Emilie Madison, and I've been treating Leah." She extends a long, slender hand toward me and I shake it. She wears a long, white coat, unbuttoned so that I can see the gray slacks and light blue button she's wearing underneath. He hair is black and wavy and there are streaks of gray running through it.

"How is she?" I ask.

"She doing well, very well in fact considering the circumstances. But her body is extremely stressed. There's not much else we can do for her except let her rest."

"Is she going to be okay?

"She'll recover. It will just take some time. She may sleep for a few days, but she'll recover." She bends down and places her hand on my shoulder. "I know you want to see her, and I want you to see her too, but I can assure you she's being taken care of. You should get some rest, and come back tomorrow." She looks at the bandage on my hand.

She was right. I haven't slept in I don't know how long. Although still agitated about not being able to see Leah, I thank the doctor for everything she's done and leave.

GRETCHEN DROPPED ME OFF at my apartment, along with my phone. She was able to convince and officer to let her have it. She can work magic sometimes. Miles had called me, told me to stop by the police station; he needed to show me something. I could also pick up my car. I tossed my phone on a chair then crawled into bed.

I tried to fall asleep, but sleep eluded me. I was restless and my mind raced, thinking about Leah, thinking about Constance and her role in all this.

The doctor said she was fine; she just needed rest.

But even with the doctor's reassurance, I still felt uneasy. I had to see her for myself.

But first I needed answers; I needed Miles to tell me what happened, what was going on.

Chapter Twenty
Luke

I CATCH A RIDE with Gretchen and we head for the police station. She leaves to retrieve Crouton and bring him back to my apartment. I knew the first thing Leah would ask me when she woke up would be if Crouton was safe.

Miles is already waiting for me when I open the door to the station. I follow him down the fluorescent-lit hallways that snake through the Milton Police Department. It's quiet. The only sound is the sliding of rubber soles against the dusty floor as we weave through corridor after corridor. We pass a few offices with their doors open—the same scene in each one: an overweight man with shiny bald heads hunched over their desks, working away on paperwork. Both Miles and I are silent the entire way. He walks behind his desk, which is still littered with papers, both crumpled and flat, and motions for me to sit. He sits down after me and clasps his hands in front of him.

"So." He says.

"So."

He exhales a deep breath out of his nose. "This isn't exactly standard protocol, but these are exactly normal circumstances."

No shit, I think to myself. *One minute I'm a suspect in the murder of my mother and the next I'm free to go, but now with Leah in the hospital and Constance in my place.*

He sucks on his lips, shakes his head.

"And, what happened," he motions between us, "only happened because, well, that's what the evidence told us."

That's the closest thing to an apology that I'll get: "I was only doing my job."

"What did you want me to see?" I prompt him, wanting to get out of here and see Leah as quickly as possible.

He opens a drawer to his right and retrieves a VHS tape.

VHS? What decade is this again?

"I'm sure you have a few questions."

"Naturally."

"But this should explain everything." He waves the video tape in the air, then stands up and walks to the wall on my left. There's a TV and a VHS player on a black, wheeled cart against the wall that blends in with the clutter of the office. First the hard plastic chairs, and now this? It seems the Milton PD has lifted much of their equipment from the local high school. That explains a lot.

He pops the video into the player, the antique gears spin and whirr as though it's struggling to play the video.

"Make sure you rewind it first. I don't want the ending to be ruined."

He ignores me, standing next to the TV, his arms folded across his waist.

An image comes into focus, but the sound is too low. Miles pushes a button on the TV and green vertical lines begin line the bottom of the screen. The chair scratches against the floor as I stand up to get a better look at the image.

It's a birds-eye view of a room, black and white. Apparently a color camera would be too much to ask from the Milton PD. Maybe I'll send a few bucks their way. There are two people in focus, but only one person's face is in view—a woman, Constance.

I don't know what question the police officer asked, but Constance is generous with her answer. It's less an answer than a story. And she keeps talking about someone named Abigail.

"Well, they took Abigail from me. You know that right? They took her from my arms and kept far away from me. They even stopped calling her Abigail. They were a rotten family. Just rotten."

"When you say, Abigail, do you mean Leah?"

"Heavens no."

"Who's Abigail?"

"My daughter of course. Haven't you been listening to a word I've said?"

Constance had a daughter? I pause the tape and ask Miles who Abigail is and what this has to do with Leah, or me for that matter.

"We looked into it. She's not lying when she says Abigail is her daughter. She did have a daughter named Abigail." He hesitates for a moment, an air of uneasiness surrounds both of us. "But she died nearly 30 years ago. When she's talking about Abigail in this video, she's really talking about Leah. She thinks Leah is her daughter."

What the fuck...

I don't even know what to think right

now, but it doesn't matter because I can't think at all. It's as though my brain has simply shut down. My mouth hangs open as I stare blankly at Miles.

He shrugs, shakes his head, then reaches out and fast forwards the tape.

"They were wicked people," Constance begins. "How could they just take my Abigail away from me? She wasn't happy there. I could tell. Some days she'd come over and I'd give her a little treat and she'd tell me about *Judith.*" There's a sharp edge to her voice when she mentions my mother's name. But then she smiles, a crooked, thin-lipped smile that looks more like a sneer than a smile. "But things always a way of sorting themselves out. And now Abigail can come live with me again. When can I see her? She's not feeling very well and she needs her medicine."

"When you say 'medicine,' what kind of medicine are you talking about?"

"Oh, this and that." There's a lightness to her voice, it's cheerful almost, as though someone asked her for a recipe after tasting a pie she baked. "It's a secret."

"How long have you been giving Leah, I mean, Abigail this medicine?"

"For years, of course!" The tone of her voice makes it clear how stupid she think the question is. She adds, "She's always been a sickly child." She looks absently off to the side, as though reminiscing with herself. "She *needs* the medicine. She *needs* me."

Miles stops the video.

"The medicine she's referring to is a wicked cocktail of anticonvulsants, barbiturates, and who knows what else. We're still trying to figure out everything else that was in Leah's system, and not to mention cataloging the small pharmacy that we found in Constance's home."

"She's been poisoning Leah?"

"Yes. For how long, we don't know. We know she's been fixated with Leah for a while now, but we can't get straight answers from her most of the time. She's caught up in this fantasy world: Leah's her ailing daughter and all this *medicine* she's feeding her is somehow *helping* her and not slowly *killing* her. I've never seen anything like it."

The more I find out about Constance, the more I'm leaning toward her as the one who poisoned Leah as a child and not Judith. I hadn't even considered Constance—why would I? She didn't have the same access to

Leah, but I guess it didn't matter. I had no idea that Leah actually visited with Constance on a somewhat consistent basis. Couple that with the fact that she believes Leah to be her daughter and it seems clear.

"Leah had concerns about Judith poisoning her. We searched the contents of her house and found bottle after bottle of herbal remedies—homeopathic medicine—nothing that could be considered harmful. There wasn't so much as an aspirin." He shakes his head. "It was night and day compared to what we found in Constance's medicine cabinet, and kitchen, and office, and well, everywhere. We found bottle after bottle of prescription pills for all sorts of ailments. Barbiturates, amphetamines, insulin, opiates, blood thinners, ketamine, anticonvulsants, antidepressants, and some really wicked stuff called succinylcholine. Things that she shouldn't have access to."

"Then how did she get them?"

"We don't know." He shrugs. "She used to be a nurse. Maybe she created her cache over the years, slowly adding to it so as to not raise suspicions. Or maybe she called in some favors. Multiple favors from multiple people. We're looking into it now."

It's hard to let go of my vision of Judith. I've placed her into this box, and even now after it's clear to me that she didn't poison Leah, nor Robert for that matter, it's hard to take her out of it. I'll always see her as a terrible human being who I believe harmed Leah more than Constance's poison.

There are antidotes for poison, ways to flush it from your system, but emotionally scarring—psychological pain—can't be flushed away in a day or two.

"We know now that Constance killed Leah. She admitted to it—in her own way—during our questioning. We can finish watching if you'd like."

I've heard and seen just about enough. Most of my questions—the important ones, at least—have been answered. And I can work out the others myself. I'm tired, pissed off at myself for not being able to protect Leah, and I just want to get out of here.

I ask for my car back. Mile's tells me where I can pick it up. He tries to apologize for arresting me; tells me it was because of the pills they found in my car, ones that turned up in the to report. I listen to part of it, but I no longer care.

I'm getting out of here.

I'm getting Leah.

Chapter Twenty-One
Leah

The next time I wake up, I'm in a hospital.

Light streams in through the window to my right and spreads a warm, goldenrod blanket across the room. There's a brown wicker basket filled with all sorts of wonderful, bright flowers on the table in front of me. There's a tingling sensation filling my core and spreading out through my body, and I feel happy.

But then I'm struck by a thought: it wasn't a dream. What I experienced, what Constance did to me was real.

A sudden urge to cut overwhelms me, and I sit up, but as I do, I realize that Luke is fast asleep next to me, his hand resting on my own. I sit there a moment, watching him as his back rises and falls with each breath. I don't want to disturb him, but my desire to see his face again wins out.

The urge to cut subsides and I grab his hand and squeeze it. He begins to stir, slowly, and after a minute or so he's up.

"Hi," I whisper.

"Hi." He smiles back at me then leans in for a hug. I wrap my arms around him and squeeze hard. I don't want to let go. I want to feel his arms around me, protecting me. I want to keep breathing in his heady, masculine scent. He begins to pull away, but I squeeze tighter.

"No."

He laughs and we continue to hug. Finally, I let go, and he pulls away and kisses me on my forehead. He sits back down in the chair next to the bed.

"How do you feel?" He asks. His eyes are red and tired; his clothes are wrinkled and it doesn't look like he's shaved in a while.

"I have a slight headache, but otherwise I feel fine. But, what about you? You look like death!"

He snorts. "Thanks. I'm well, now that I know you are." I can feel myself blush. I've nearly forgotten all about Constance, but there's a part of me that's wondering what happened after I blacked out again.

"If you want to talk about, you know, we can."

I didn't want to remember being strapped to a bed. I didn't want to think about Constance, but I knew I would have to face it eventually. If I swept it away, I'd feel better for a little while. But something like this won't just stay locked away. Things like this, pain like this will manifest itself in other ways. No. I had to face it now. I asked Luke to tell me happened after I blacked out.

Luke recounts what he learned from Miles and the video of Constance's questioning. It was a relief to know that Gretchen heard my cries for help, but everything else he tells me is awful, absolutely horrible. But I guess it wasn't anything I didn't already know. I knew she believed that I was her daughter, but it frightened me just how far she went to try and make it happen, her own sick, twisted reality. She had no qualms killing Judith. But something didn't sit right with me.

"Why did she kill Judith?" I ask.

"I've been thinking about that. The best explanation I can come up with is that it was her last resort. I mean, she saw you as her end goal—she'd do anything to have you.

I'm certain now that it was Constance, not Judith who poisoned you when you were a child. Miles searched Judith's house. All it turned up was herbal remedies, homeopathic medicine that wouldn't cure a runny nose let alone harm you. Constance, on the other hand, had a small pharmacy worth of drugs.

She poisoned you, as far as I can tell, to raise suspicions over Judith and Robert's parenting. 'Why does Leah keep getting sick, and why does she get better when she's out of her mother's care?' It was her attempt to remove you from their home, and hopefully place you in hers. She was trying to play the part of the nice, old lady who would just love to foster an abused child.

It didn't work out that way though. You went to Millwood and she no longer had access to you. But that didn't stop her. She switched her target: Robert. He started getting sick just as you were, leaving Judith to be even more suspicious. I have to say it worked. Everything was pointing to Judith. So when I learned about Robert's death, I suspected Judith and came back for you.

When she overheard my argument with Judith, she saw a chance to kill two birds with one stone, so to speak: kill Judith and pin the murder on me. She knew I needed certain pills, and that I carried those pills around with me. She was a nurse, so she could have easily found what pills I took by calling in a favor, or by even asking Judith. She made sure that were in Judith's system when she killed her. It wouldn't have been difficult. She probably went over there after I left, crushed the pills and put them in a snack or drink, and fed it to Judith. Then she did what she did best. She killed Judith. Probably with the succinylcholine. It would've been the easiest method. Just little injection when Judith was busy."

I don't know what to say. It was clear that Luke had given it a lot of thought and from what I understood, it made sense. But that doesn't mean that I believed it. I hate to think that there are people like Judith in this world.

It was too exhausting to think about. I fell back against the pillows and closed my eyes.

"Too much?" Luke asks.

"No. I mean, kind of. It's just a lot to take in." I take a deep breath and exhale. "But I think you're right."

I can hear Luke move away from me and

walk to the table at the end of the bed. There's a sound of plastic crinkling, something sliding off of the table, followed by the striking of a match.

"Happy Birthday to you..." Luke sings.

I laugh and open my eyes. "What? It's my birthday?"

"Well, not quite. It's tomorrow. I wasn't sure when you were going to wake up, but I wanted to have a treat for you when you did."

It was so sweet and thoughtful; I wanted to squeal right then and there.

He brings the slice of cake over to me. "Make a wish."

I wish for happiness. I wish for me to leave Milton and never return. I wish for a new life with Luke and me (and of course Crouton!) far away from here.

I take a deep breath and blow out the candle and with it the painful life I've been living.

CHAPTER TWENTY-TWO
LEAH

April 8th, 2014

It's funny how life can change so quickly, for better or worse. In the past few months, I've been lucky; my life has changed for the better and in ways I never could've imagined.

Right now, for instance. I'm sitting here, writing this entry, at a large oak desk in a penthouse suite that overlooks the heart of Tokyo.

There's a gentle breeze that flutters my hair every now and then, coming in from the open door that leads to the veranda. Luke is standing out there, his arms perched on the edge of the railing, holding something— what exactly, I can't tell. His back is to me, but I can imagine his face. I can picture the way his eyes soften as he smiles, the slight wrinkle of his nose, the single dimple on his left cheek.

I just gave myself goosebumps. My heart still races whenever I think about Luke—a feeling I hope will never fade.

But enough of that...

I'm in Tokyo... Japan!

I never thought I'd travel anywhere. Definitely not outside of the country or out of Texas for that matter. But I am out of Texas and out of Milton. And surprisingly, this isn't my first time.

It seems like every month Luke is whisking me away on another adventure. Paris. London. Milan. Been there. Done that. India? New Zealand? Thailand? Check, check, and check. Those are only a few of the places. I can't even remember them all!

My life is surreal; it's a dream I couldn't even imagine living less than a year ago—or ever. But here I am, sitting in a luxurious penthouse, high above the Tokyo skyline, without a care in the world. The possibilities seem endless.

My life with Luke, although with its own set of ups and downs has, overall, been amazing.

I'm working for him now! His assistant. It has its own sets of ups and downs, but I enjoy working closely with Luke, even though he can be a real asshole sometimes.

I remember my first day on the job. He takes me into the office, and of course he immediately tries to undress me. I'd like to say I stopped him. I mean, having sex in his office? On my first day? It was wrong, but I can't say I didn't enjoy it. And the next time it happened… and the time after… Okay, you get the point.

I love Luke. And these past few months have been some of the happiest I've ever had.

I'm actually happy. It's so strange writing those words, but it's the truth. I'm happy

Even with all the terrible things that happened, I think everything turned out alright. Constance is spending however much time she has left in a psychiatric hospital, like Millwood, but for violent offenders.

I know some people might think I'm crazy—after everything Constance put me and my family through—but I can't help but feel sorry for her.

I've been told that time heals all wounds, but I'm not sure that's true. I think that there are some wounds that can't be healed by time. Sure, the pain from most wounds can disappear over time, or at the very least diminish. But when I think about this, and then think about Constance, I know for certain that it isn't true. It's more like, 'time can heal most wounds.'

I can't imagine what it would be like to lose a child. As a nurse, Constance spent her life helping sick people, mending them. But when it came to her own daughter, her own flesh and blood, there was nothing she could do. And that affected her deeply. A hole opened up inside her and no matter how much time passed, no matter how hard she tried to plug it with alcohol and other distractions, it remained. Deepened, even.

When I came along, she saw me as the solution. The answer she could never find. And well, the rest is history.

I could be angry about what she did, about all the pain she put me through. I could scream and yell from the highest tower, from mountaintops, about how evil and fucked up it was that she did that to me. I have. But it doesn't change anything. It doesn't make me feel any better.

Time has passed; the wound is beginning to heal. There's still more healing to go, but the pain no longer consumes me. Now, when I think about, which isn't very often, I feel sorry for Constance. She loved her daughter dearly, and through her own twisted logic, did all she could to make things right. Fill the gap in her heart.

I'll be the first to concede that what she did was wrong, fucked up—whatever—, but I can, in some way, understand it.

But, it's all behind me now.

I haven't thought about cutting in nearly a year; I haven't used my rubber bands in that same time. I don't need them anymore. I have Luke. I have my job. And, of course, Crouton! But most importantly, I've found happiness. That's all that matters now.

Look at me. Droning on and on. I told Luke I'd only be a few minutes, but I've been at it for nearly an hour! He's still out there on the veranda, but I'm sure he's wondering what's taking me so long.

I guess I should wrap it up. And I will because I just remembered the incredible meal Luke has in store for us. There's this sushi restaurant that you have to reserve a spot months in advance. A friend of his at work (who made the initial reservation) couldn't make it, so he offered it to Luke a few weeks ago. I jumped at the chance. I've never had sushi before, but lately I've been adamant about trying something new as often as possible. It's refreshing and makes me feel alive, knowing that there is still so much to do, so much to learn about and live.

I've been painting a lot lately and recently I've been enthralled by the Japanese art and culture. The cherry blossoms are in bloom and I pestered Luke until he finally agreed to take me. We saw them today! They were even more beautiful than I could imagine. I can die happy.

Honestly, I don't know how this day could get any better. But I am curious about what else he has in store for me.

He's been secretive about everything else we're going to do on this trip (what else is new?), but I know it will be fun either way. Luke always knows what I like, and I haven't been disappointed yet.

Well, I guess that's it for now! Off for some (hopefully) delicious sushi! Half a year wait? It better be...

Chapter Twenty-Three
Luke

When I think about Leah, I think of her resiliency more than anything else. I've never known a stronger person—someone who can endure so many painful experiences but still bounce back with a smile. I can feel my own mouth turn into a smile as I picture her smiling face.

It's a playful smile, with a childlike quality to it—innocent. I can picture the way she tilts her head, the right side of her mouth beginning to curl as she looks away, bashful yet beautiful. A soft pink hue begins to color her cheeks just before she looks up at me. Her eyebrows shoot up as the left corner of her mouth catches up with her right, forming her delicate and sweet smile.

In moments like this, I'm powerless. I have no other option but to wrap my arms around her, pull her into me, and kiss her. She forces me to. Honest.

I'm standing out on our suite's veranda, watching the mass of cars and people swarm the Tokyo streets below. We've been in Japan for a few days, seeing some of the sights—Mount Fuji is absolutely stunning—and eating more fresh seafood than you can imagine. Leah's behind me, writing a journal entry. She's been writing in that journal of hers religiously, but she won't share anything she's written and that's okay.

We all have our own secrets, things we want to keep private. It's human nature.

She tells me it's to help with the healing process. It seems to be working. Seeing her happy makes me happy.

This high in the sky, the sounds of the city merge into a low hum as they filter up to me. It's relaxing, this birds-eye view of things, and I'm completely relaxed. My mind is clear of distractions and I can think.

And lately, I've been thinking about us —Leah and I. Us—the dreaded "us." The "us" that, until now, I thought I'd never want. Why would I want to settle down when there are so many beautiful women out there? I could have a new one each night, and before Leah, I did.

But, things change; *people* change. That

style of living can be exciting for a time, but it wears you down. After everything I've been through with Leah, I've gained a much needed, different perspective on my life. My goals have shifted. I want other things. Well, one thing: Leah.

I take a small black box from my pocket. It's not very large—it doesn't need to be to hold what's inside. It's iconic, the box. Take one out anywhere and you'll know what's inside. It might look different, not what you'd expect, but the message and meaning it carries remains the same.

For me, it means farewell to the life I used to lead. And not in a bad way. I'm not dragging my feet, longing for the bachelor life. Quite the opposite.

It's an amicable parting of ways from a life that no longer suits me. We've grown apart these past few months and I need something else, someone else. Onward and upward to new and greater things.

My fingers trace the exterior of the black box. The box springs open without much effort and I glance at its contents one last time. It's still there, the ring. I agonized for months over which ring would be perfect. Yes, I've known Leah was the one for a while now. I wanted the ring to be perfect. I went with something classic, elegant, something simple yet sophisticated. I know she's going to love it.

I've had the ring for a few months now, held in my pocket, waiting for the perfect moment.

But is there a perfect moment?

The more I think about it, the more I realize that there isn't a perfect moment; that you could spend your entire life waiting for it, waiting for all the planets to align and angels to descend from heaven, heralding the moment as perfect, only to realize that your life passed you by; that you spent more time waiting—analyzing every detail and situation—than you did living.

No. I don't believe there are perfect moments, and if there are, I doubt anyone would be able to recognize one. But I believe we can come close to making them ourselves. And I think that's a beautiful thing.

I can hear the clack of Leah's heels against the concrete as she walks across the veranda. I close the box and slip it back into my pocket just before she wraps her arms around my waist.

"I'm sorry it took so long. I got carried away, I guess." Her voice is sweet and soft and she smells like jasmine and lavender. She rests her head against my back.

"Not a problem." I smile. "It's nice out here." I can feel her head lift from my back as she looks out from where we're standing. The Tokyo skyline is slowly swallowing the blood-orange sun, leaving the sky blotted with swaths of pinks, oranges, and reds.

She steps beside me, one arm still wrapped around my waist. I place my left hand along the small of her back and watch her as she gazes at the setting sun. Stray tendrils of her chestnut curls flutter against her cheek from the gentle breeze and her skin looks golden in the sunlight.

"Have you ever seen something so beautiful before?"

"Yes."

"What?" She hasn't taken her eyes off the sunset and her voice seems to drift to me, carried by light breeze. I lift my hand from the small of her back, brush the stray tendril off her face, push it behind her ear and tell her, "You."

She snorts and shakes her head.

"That's so cheesy." She's quiet for a

moment but then says, "I like it, though. And I like this. Us. Watching the sunset. Everything about it. It's more than I could ask for. It's—"

"Perfect," I interject as I finger the box in my pocket.

My mind goes blank. All I see is Leah beautiful face looking down at me as I kneel before her, her wrapped in mine. I ask her the one question I'll never ask another person again.

And through a tearful smile, she responds with a single, beautiful word.

"Yes."

From the Author

Thank you so much for taking the time to read my story. It means a lot to me. I hope you enjoyed reading it as much as I enjoyed writing it. If you have the time, please consider leaving an honest review by clicking here. I would love to hear what you liked (or didn't like!) about the story.

If you would like read more stories by me, you can sign up for my mailing list. I send out emails whenever I publish something new.

Thank you again!

Click here to sign

up for Lillian Thorne's mailing list.

Printed in Great Britain
by Amazon